SEQUESTERED
HEARTS

Visit us at www.boldstrokesbooks.com

What Reviewers Say About BOLD STROKES Authors

KIM BALDWIN

"*Force of Nature* is filled with nonstop, fast paced action. Tornadoes, raging fire blazes, heroic and daring rescues…Baldwin does a fine job of describing the fast-paced scenes and inspiring the reader to keep on turning the pages." – L-word.comLiterature

ROSE BEECHAM

"…her characters seem fully capable of walking away from the particulars of whodunit and engaging the reader in other aspects of their lives." – *Lambda Book Report*

GEORGIA BEERS

"Beers weaves a tale of yearning, love, lust, and conflict resolution. She has constructed a believable plot, with strong characters in a charming setting." – *JustAboutWrite*

RONICA BLACK

"*Wild Abandon* tells how these two women come to realize that 'life was too precious to be ruled by…fears, by…demons.' While these two women struggle with their issues, there is some very, very hot sex. If you enjoy complex characters and passionate sex scenes, you'll love *Wild Abandon.*" – *MegaScene*

GUN BROOKE

"*Course of Action* is a romance…populated with a host of captivating and amiable characters. The glimpses into the lifestyles of the rich and beautiful people are rather like guilty pleasures…a most satisfying and entertaining reading experience." – *Midwest Book Review*

CATE CULPEPPER

"…an exceptional storyteller who has taken on a very difficult subject …and turned it into a spellbinding novel. As an author, she understands well that fiction can teach us our own history." – *JustAboutWrite*

JANE FLETCHER

"*The Exile and the Sorcerer* is a mesmerizing read, a tour-de-force packed with adventure, ordeals, complex twists and turns, and the internal introspection of appealing characters." – *Midwest Book Review*

JD GLASS

"*Punk Like Me*…is different. It is engaging. It is life-affirming. Frankly, it is genius. This is a rare book in that it has a soul; one that is laid bare for all to see." – *JustAboutWrite*

GRACE LENNOX

"*Chance* is refreshing…Every nuance is powerful and succinct. *Chance* is not a novel about the music industry; it is about a woman discovering herself as she muddles through all the trappings of fame." – *Midwest Book Review*

LEE LYNCH

"Lynch, with a dozen novels to her credit dating back to the early days of Naiad Press, has earned her stripes as a writerly elder. She was contributing stories to the lesbian magazine *The Ladder* four decades ago. But this latest is sublimely in tune with the times." – *Q-Syndicate*

JLEE MEYER

"*Forever Found*…neatly combines hot sex scenes, humor, engaging characters, and an exciting story." – *MegaScene*

RADCLYFFE

"…well-plotted…lovely romance…I couldn't turn the pages fast enough!" – Ann Bannon, author of *The Beebo Brinker Chronicles*

SUSAN SMITH

"This disparate duo's lush rush of a romance - which incorporates reincarnation, a grounded transman and his peppy daughter, and the dark moods of a troubled witch - pays wonderful homage to Leslie Feinberg's classic gender-bending novel, *Stone Butch Blues*." – *Q-Syndicate*

ALI VALI

"Rich in character portrayal, *The Devil Inside* by Ali Vali is an unusual, unpredictable, and thought-provoking love story that will have the reader questioning the definition of right and wrong long after she finishes the book." – *JustAboutWrite*

SEQUESTERED
HEARTS

by

Erin Dutton

2007

SEQUESTERED HEARTS

© 2007 BY ERIN DUTTON. ALL RIGHTS RESERVED.

ISBN: 10-DIGIT 1-933110-78-3
       13-DIGIT 978-1-933110-78-3

THIS TRADE PAPERBACK ORIGINAL IS PUBLISHED BY
BOLD STROKES BOOKS, INC.,
NEW YORK, USA

FIRST EDITION: MAY 2007.

CREDITS
EDITORS: JENNIFER KNIGHT AND STACIA SEAMAN
PRODUCTION DESIGN: STACIA SEAMAN
COVER DESIGN BY SHERI (GRAPHICARTIST2020@HOTMAIL.COM)

Acknowledgments

Thanks to Radclyffe, for giving me the opportunity to do so many things that I never dreamed I would do. You have created a nurturing and supportive atmosphere and you lead by example. I am such a fan of both the author and the publisher.

Editors Jennifer Knight and Stacia Seaman were instrumental in making this book the very best it could be. Jennifer, your lessons have not only added another dimension to this story, but will enrich my future work as well.

Sheri, the cover is amazing. And thank you to everyone else at Bold Strokes Books—what a great place to be!

I need to thank my family. You have supported me through every decision I have made, even when they led me further from you. I love you.

Finally, Scott, through the years and through the miles, our friendship is ever present.

Dedication

In memory of Brandon Keith Davis.
I miss you every day.

Chapter One

"A re you sure you're ready for this?"

Cori Saxton sighed. Her agent and good friend Gretchen had asked the same question several times during today's conversation. Tucking the phone between her ear and her shoulder, she leaned back and balanced her chair precariously on two legs. She had been lounging on the deck at the rear of her house, trying to soak in a few hours of solitude before her tranquility was destroyed by a reporter from *Canvassed* magazine.

She didn't get outdoors often enough, Cori reflected, staring out across her sloping back lawn. A fieldstone path wound through expertly manicured grass the color of deep emeralds. Midway down the path she'd created a small sitting area with stone benches and shade trees.

She'd owned the fifty acres in upstate New York for almost five years, having fallen in love with both the property and the house the first time she'd seen it. She was visiting the previous owner, an architect friend who had designed and built the house for his wife. Sadly, they didn't get to enjoy their dream retreat for long. Carol had died of cancer only two years after its completion and Anthony decided he could no longer live in their home without her. When Cori heard he was looking to sell, she'd jumped at the chance.

The edge of her property ran to the riverbank, where a sizable dock housed her latest acquisition, a Chaparral Signature 276 she'd purchased earlier in the spring. She had only taken the sleek white craft out a few times. It had been an impulse purchase. She'd seen a similar boat in the marina last year and simply had to have one. It wasn't hard to justify the extravagance; her last day sailer had been fine for the short visits that were all she'd ever managed to arrange, but things were different now.

She'd had big plans for the upstate hideaway, but it was hard to justify time out when her career had finally taken off. She was expected to maintain a certain degree of visibility and her plans had fallen by the wayside. In the past few years, she had rarely gotten the opportunity to spend more than a weekend at a time here. *Not anymore,* she thought wryly. For once her life was her own and she was going to stay out of town for as long as she wanted. Today's interview was the one concession she was willing to make right now, and only because she had her own ideas about how the interview was going to work.

Cori checked her wristwatch and glanced down at her tank top and nylon running shorts. Her unwelcome visitor was due in just a couple of hours. She supposed she should go indoors, take a shower, and change into clothing suitable for an heiress-turned-artist.

"Well," Gretchen demanded.

"They're just going to keep calling until I give them something," Cori finally answered. "Besides, the interview was your idea. Now you're trying to talk me out of it?"

"I know. I guess I was just worried that maybe I had pushed you into it. What are you going to say?"

"I'll think of something." In fact, she had already settled on the carefully constructed fiction she wanted this reporter to circulate. Apart from Gretchen, very few people knew the truth behind her self-imposed exile, and she intended to keep it that way.

"Well, be careful," Gretchen warned. "You know Mitchell Gardner. He's not going to send a junior out to interview you."

"I know, I know." Cori searched her memory for the name she'd seen in the e-mail confirming the date and time of arrival at the airport. "The guy is a freelancer. Bennett McClain. Henry is picking him up at the airport."

Henry and his wife Alma owned the property next to hers, and she'd hired them to look after her house and grounds during her long absences. Alma stocked the pantry when Cori was planning a visit, and Henry helped her out with odd jobs and errands while she was there.

She'd felt a little guilty asking him to collect her visitor today, but she was aware that, being retired, he and Alma could use the income these small services provided. And besides, the last thing she wanted was to be stuck in a car with this reporter for a forty-minute drive.

"Don't worry about me," she told Gretchen. "I have everything under control."

"Don't forget who you're talking to. I know just how out of control you feel right now." Gretchen's voice softened. "Call me if you need anything. And make nice with him. Okay?"

"I'll work on it." Smiling, Cori hung up. She wasn't exactly known for her tact when dealing with the media, but this time she intended to try.

Weeks of continuous questioning about her supposed disappearance had grated on her nerves, and giving some kind of answer seemed like the best way to put an end to the speculation, once and for all. She really didn't understand what the big deal was anyway. She'd only been out of circulation for two months, yet everyone was acting like the art world had stopped because she was no longer a fixture at every gathering. Had she been so completely defined by her social activities that no one could understand her just needing a break?

Even as she asked herself the question she knew the answer. She had. And the truth was, it was more than just needing a break that had sent her running from her life.

Forcing herself out of her deck chair, she went into the kitchen and refilled her iced tea then wandered into her spacious living room. Large expanses of floor-to-ceiling glass along its northeastern wall let in natural light as well as affording a perfect view of the river. Cori had furnished the room in varying shades of olive and taupe, accented with deep purples. The hardwood floors had been stripped and refinished to a warm honeyed oak. She sank down into her favorite sofa, a surprisingly comfortable piece despite its minimalist lines, and gazed out at the river, taking stock of her life.

Normally, she tended to avoid idle reflection even when she

felt stressed. She preferred to distract herself from her problems and never had any trouble finding someone willing to party, especially if it was on her dime. She also had enough of a perspective on reality to know that most of the planet would be thrilled to have "problems" like hers. Cori had been born into privilege and was well aware of how easy that made her life in most of the ways that mattered. Her family's money and stature was long established. As a child, she had heard the phrase "the Connecticut Saxtons" attached to her name so many times that she was nine years old before she realized that not everyone had their families referenced that way.

High school had taught her that her parents' name afforded her the freedom to do exactly as she pleased with little consequence, and she had taken full advantage of that fact. Only recently had she begun to understand that never having to take responsibility for anything meant missing out on some key learning experiences, among them that money and good looks could only get you so far, and some things were completely out of your control.

Cori's mind drifted to the reason for her seclusion, then just as quickly retreated as anger and helplessness flooded her. In hindsight, she could see that being an only child hadn't taught her how to deal with pressure any more than it had taught her the give-and-take of intimacy with other people. She was far too used to having everything her way. Her every whim had been indulged by her parents, and she'd quickly learned that even if she couldn't rely on her family name for a free pass, her looks carried a certain amount of weight.

Contemplating the past few years, she was suddenly painfully aware that she had wasted time she could have spent much more productively, time she would never get back. It had never crossed her mind that she would one day nurse regrets about the lifestyle she'd enjoyed since her teens.

The partying ways that had begun in high school had continued through college and over the years that followed graduation. She had spent a year in Paris, studying art at École des Beaux-Arts and having lovers in various European cities. Cori had never made any secret of her escapades, much to her mother's consternation. Her father, however, didn't seem bothered by the accounts of her success with women. That had never surprised her. Adam Saxton wasn't concerned with anyone's opinion about him. It was one of the few points they agreed on—that and their passion for their respective livelihoods. But her father's idea of success was measured in dollar signs, which made it difficult for him to understand Cori's artistic ambitions. Still, he tried. He'd even attended a few of her shows, and one of her more sedate pieces occupied a place of honor in his office.

Cori's mother had always been the one who worried about appearances. Catherine Saxton had been born into society life and had done her best to groom her daughter for the same. Cori's resistance to her efforts was a constant source of conflict between them, and her refusal to hide her sexuality stretched the limits of her mother's tolerance on a regular basis.

Catherine had even gone so far as to suggest Cori marry an acceptable young man and carry on her affairs with women discreetly on the side. At the time, Cori had laughed off the idea as absurd and made sure she was photographed the next night in an obvious clinch with the daughter of a prominent local politician. Flirting just on the safe side of her mother's disapproval was second nature. Catherine pushed and Cori pushed back, and in the end they would agree to disagree.

This delicate balance was upset when Cori sat her mother down just before the latest trip upstate and told her the truth about her present situation. It had been Gretchen's idea; she was always trying tactful interventions to bring them closer together. *You only have one mother. Unconditional love is a gift.* Cori could repeat the lectures in her sleep. She supposed the conversation had gone as well as could be expected. Her mother had cried and then railed against the medical profession. By the end of the conversation she'd decided that what was really lacking was adequate funding for research. Cori had spent the next thirty minutes talking her mother out of organizing a fund-raising dinner. She now treated Cori with kid gloves, acting as if she was fragile and avoiding confrontation at all cost. Cori was stunned. It seemed this one aspect of who she was suddenly defined her completely; she couldn't even count on her own mother to treat her as if she was normal. Would she spend the rest of her life being viewed as damaged?

Cori set her iced tea on the nearest coffee table, swung her legs up onto the sofa, and settled back into the deep cushioning with her eyes closed. She kept expecting to wake up one morning and find her life was just the same as it had been for most of her twenty-nine years. Today was the first day she'd truly understood that wasn't going to happen and even if it did, something in her had changed. She would not be able to pick up exactly where she left off, even if she wanted to. And lately she wasn't so sure she did.

❖

As the Beechcraft twin-engine turboprop lurched in the turbulent sky, Bennett McClain's stomach went with it. She'd looked up her destination, Ogdensburg, on the Internet the night before and was not surprised to find a small dot that was barely even on the map along the upper edge of New York state. *Christ, from the map I could barely tell if the place was still in New York or in Canada.* So she shouldn't have been surprised when she changed planes in Syracuse and found her next mode of transportation was propeller-driven.

Staring out the window, she wondered once again how she had let herself get talked into this assignment. She'd been dead set against it from the moment she'd heard the details from Mitchell Gardner, senior editor of *Canvassed*, an up-and-coming art magazine she'd written a couple of features for. The only reason she had even agreed to entertain the possibility was that Mitchell was a good friend. She still couldn't understand why he was so determined to run with a piece on Cori Saxton.

In the past five years, the woman had gained fame as a gifted artist. Ben had read various flattering reviews about her work and her talent, and had always wondered just how much the Saxton name contributed to the breathless awe of these pieces. Descriptions such as "edgy" and "brave" were routinely applied to her paintings, and the art establishment seemed to have reached the consensus that she was "brilliant." Of course her hard-living, reckless lifestyle had attracted almost as much publicity as her art, and it seemed Cori never shied from a camera, even when it caught her in a compromising position with one woman or another.

Ben wasn't alone in wondering when the woman found time for painting, but Cori Saxton's detractors were silenced when, with each successive show, her pieces seemed to surpass those of the last. Strangely, the self-promoting artist hadn't been seen at any of her customary haunts in two months. Ben wasn't losing any sleep over her disappearance. It made a pleasant change not to see the usual society pages shots of her at this party or that with a drink in her hand and a glassy look in her eyes.

"So what?" she'd told Mitchell when he dragged her into his office to pester her to do the story. "She's probably in rehab or something, and I don't write gossip column stuff."

"As if I would ask." Mitchell acted wounded. "There's a story here, Ben. Everyone knows Cori Saxton wouldn't just drop off the face of the earth for no good reason."

"Maybe she wants some privacy for a change," Ben suggested, doubting it. Publicity was oxygen for women like Cori. Without it they wilted. This had to be some kind of stunt. Maybe she'd decided to reinvent herself as reclusive and mysterious, only to find that got old after a few weeks and she now needed to be the center of attention again.

"If she wants privacy all she needs to do is say so," Mitchell said snippily. "The fact that she won't even make a statement through her publicist means everyone wants to break this one. And the good news is," he smiled arrogantly, "we're the people she's going to talk to."

"What makes you think that?" Ben asked.

"I have a friend who knows her agent. To make a long story short, Saxton agreed to an exclusive with *Canvassed*." He rushed on before she could respond. "She wants final approval. She says it's a deal breaker—"

"You have to be kidding me." Ben was ready to walk out. She had not spent the past ten years building a reputation as a first-rate journalist to have her work rewritten until it read like a lame puff piece. Mitchell knew that, and he should have thought about it before he called her.

He waved at her to sit down. "Ben, hear me out."

"I said no. I will not do a story contingent upon the subject's approval. I don't have to do that anymore, Mitch."

These days she didn't have to take assignments she didn't want and she didn't have to write to please someone else. She had no plans to be used as a mouthpiece by a spoiled socialite turned "artist." If that's what Cori Saxton was looking for, she was going to be disappointed.

Mitch wasn't about to let her out the door. "Ben, the magazine is not doing as well as projected. I really need this, and you're the only one I trust to get me a decent story even with her right of approval. I'm asking you for a favor."

His gently pleading tone kept Ben in her seat, against her better judgment, listening to him map out the details. Mitchell had sunk his life savings into this magazine. Ben couldn't let him lose it without trying to help. They'd known each other for thirteen years, and in that time he'd always helped her out as she built her career.

Knowing she would regret it, she had relented in the end, and now, less than a week later, she was on the smallest plane she had ever seen, headed for God knows where to attempt to interview a woman she gathered was suddenly allergic to publicity but still couldn't fade happily into anonymity. Mitchell had given her a file containing background on Cori, a plane ticket, and instructions to stay as long as she needed to in order to get the right stuff.

Cynically, she thought ten minutes would probably suffice for the life story of Cori Saxton. As for whatever spin the woman wanted to put on her exodus from the city, Ben could hardly wait to hear it. So far this week, she hadn't seen enough television to get her fill of banality. She was counting on her subject to remedy that.

CHAPTER TWO

B en descended the few steps of the plane, happy to be on solid ground once again. She waited patiently planeside until her bag was handed to her. As she walked toward the terminal she surveyed the small airport. There was only one runway and the building she entered was little more than a large room with some airport equipment scattered about. An x-ray machine stood along one wall, separated from the rest of the room by a metal detector. A long counter stood between her and the lone reservation clerk. An older man had just approached the clerk, and Ben couldn't help but overhear his words.

"I'm looking for a Mr. Bennett McClain." He had glanced at her as she entered but dismissed her, obviously expecting a man. Quite used to this type of misunderstanding, Ben made her way across the room.

"Excuse me, I'm sorry to interrupt but, I'm Bennett McClain," she introduced herself politely, extending her hand.

"Oh, I'm sorry, miss. I don't know why, but I was expecting..." His voice trailed off in embarrassment as he grasped her hand warmly. "Henry Rollins. I'm here to pick you up."

Ben judged him to be in his early sixties. His hairline had receded, leaving a wispy gray fringe clinging to the back and sides. Despite the day's comfortable temperature, he wore a thick flannel shirt and navy Dickies. He reached for her bag, taking it from her before she could protest. Judging from the calloused hand that brushed hers, he didn't shy away from hard work. She did manage to hold on to the laptop case, which she slung over her shoulder. She followed him outside to an older model Ford pick-up with blue paint that had begun to give way to a rusty hue. He lifted her bag easily over the tailgate, depositing it carefully in the bed of the truck next to some supplies.

"I was in town running errands, so Ms. Saxton asked me to come and fetch you," he explained as he opened the passenger door of the pick-up. He waited while she climbed inside.

"Are we far from her home?" Ben inquired casually as he slid behind the wheel.

"About forty-five minutes." He cranked the ignition and the old truck sputtered to life.

There didn't seem to be any air-conditioning in the rumbling vehicle. Henry left the windows down and the wind whipped in and tugged at Ben's loose, shoulder-length hair. Pulling her sunglasses down from the top of her head to cover her eyes, she stared out her window. They very quickly left the small town behind, the concrete and buildings giving way to open fields. Lush green grass rolled away from the side of the road, interrupted only by the occasional tree line.

There were no subdivisions here. Private homes sat on large plots of land; sometimes miles of road passed before Ben saw the next home. Compared with the city, she even noticed a subtle difference in the smell of the air that circulated through the cab of the truck, though she would have been hard pressed to find exactly the right word for it. "Fresher," maybe, but that didn't describe it fully.

Henry remained quiet, apparently feeling no need to fill the silence between them. Ben was thankful. She wasn't really in the mood for making idle conversation with a stranger. Her mind wandered back to her cousin Lucy's reaction to the news of this assignment. Insanely jealous was an understatement. As soon as Lucy had discovered the subject of Ben's latest article, she all but offered to pay Ben to bring her along as an assistant.

"Cori Saxton is just about the sexiest thing I've ever seen," she'd gushed as they polished off cartons of Chinese takeout a few days earlier.

Ben looked forward to their weekly lunches in Lucy's office, and she knew Lucy did too. Though technically they were cousins, they'd been raised virtually as sisters. Ben had spent much of her childhood under the care of her aunt Meg while her mother worked.

Lucy pulled a publicity photo out of the folder Ben had been leafing through and pushed it in front of Ben's face. "I mean, look at her."

Ben looked. Actually, she'd stared. The picture was a head shot, the type that was sent out in the press packets to advertise upcoming shows. Cori's short, dark blond hair was boyishly cut to frame an angular face that lent her features a sharpness softened only by luminous blue eyes and thick lashes resting against her cheek. It was a good photo, Ben had to admit. Her heart rate had quickened as she studied the smoldering look in Cori's eyes. Cynically, Ben decided that was precisely the effect the photographer had been going for.

"So she's attractive. So are a thousand other women." She'd handed the photo back to Lucy, ignoring her cousin's incredulous stare and trying to rationalize her own reaction to Cori's intense expression.

Now, on her way to Cori's home, she wondered if she would experience the same shock of awareness when she met the woman face-to-face. Highly unlikely. A posed photograph was simply the record of a face frozen in a single moment, everything predetermined. Cori had carefully created the image she wanted others to see, arranging her features as the photographer had instructed. In real life no one could manufacture a pose 24/7.

Ben's attention was wrenched back to the road ahead when Henry made a sharp turn off the main highway. She grabbed the door and held on as the truck lurched down what appeared to be a dirt road that wound its way among the thick stand of trees. *Is this even a road?* She tightened her fingers on the door frame as the old truck bumped along the ruts in the road.

The tree limbs on either side of the pick-up seemed frighteningly close to their windows, and the deep potholes made the vehicle sway even closer to an imminent collision. Despite the looming hazards, Henry calmly negotiated his way between the larger holes and grooves in the road. Ben had the impression he could drive it in his sleep if he had to.

Several long minutes later, she sighed with relief as he maneuvered around a sharp bend, and through a clearing in the trees a sprawling house came into view. From the front, it appeared to comprise only one story; however, the land sloped sharply away from the front of the house and over a hill and Ben guessed there was a lower level on the back side. A circular drive passed by the front before looping back to connect to the road on which they had entered.

Henry pulled the truck to a stop in front of the house, and Ben looked up to find the silhouette of a woman standing in the open doorway. She pushed open the truck door and slid out. As she started for the rear of the pick-up and her suitcase, Henry said, "Leave it, I'll bring it in later."

Before she could utter a protest, he had her by the arm and was leading her toward the house. As they reached the front entrance, the woman waiting for them opened the screen door she'd been standing behind.

With an air of formality that seemed at odds with his attire and decrepit vehicle, Henry said, "Ms. Saxton, may I present Ms. Bennett McClain."

Surprise registered momentarily on Cori Saxton's face before it was quickly replaced by a polite mask. As she stepped into the sunlight and extended her hand, Ben barely stifled a gasp. *Intense? Yes, that's the proper word for this woman.*

Cori's photos failed to do her justice. In person, she was absolutely striking. Her sharp cheekbones and strong jawline lent her a slightly chiseled look. The only break in the clean lines of her face was the indent at the tip of her chin, a feature that merely added to the appeal of an already stunning visage. Her blond hair sported sun-bleached highlights, and her skin was evenly tanned, making her blue eyes seem to glow. Somehow Ben knew the rich color did not come from a tanning bed or a bottle. Cori's body was lean, perhaps a little on the thin side, and she had at least four inches on Ben's five foot five frame.

"Ms. Saxton." Ben realized she was staring and quickly grasped Cori's outstretched hand. It's very nice to meet you."

"I thought you were a man," Cori stated bluntly, dropping her hand after the barest polite squeeze.

Ben smiled at her unapologetic tone. Flexing her tingling fingers, she said, "I get that a lot. But I assure you, I am not."

No, she certainly is not. Cory allowed her eyes to rake quickly over Ben's body. She had been expecting a male reporter and was searching her mind to recall where she'd gotten that impression. Obviously she'd been mistaken. The woman who stood before her now was not the least bit masculine. She wore a pale yellow blouse that molded nicely to her curves and was tucked into neatly pressed khaki pants. Long, thick brown hair fell in waves to her shoulders. High cheekbones and sharply arched brows lent a refined air to her soft features.

Cori let her eyes linger on Bennett McClain's full lips. *Yes, very inviting.* All in all, Bennett was attractive in a wholesome way that Cori wasn't accustomed to noticing. Before she gave herself away, she recovered her manners. "Please come in. Henry will bring your things after he unloads the truck." She held the door open, waiting until Bennett preceded her into the house.

Ben stepped into an airy foyer that opened to a living room flooded with natural light. Drawn to the view, she quickly crossed the room and looked out the windows. A large cedar deck wrapped around the back of the house, accessible by sliding doors to the left of the living room. Stairs off the rear of the deck led to a stone patio around an in-ground swimming pool. Ben had been correct about the sharply sloping lawn. The trees had been cleared all the way to the bank of a river Ben hadn't known was there. A stone path snaked its way through beautiful landscaping, back and forth across the lawn, easing the incline of land. The path ran all the way to the shore. A dock extended into the water with a white boat tied off next to it.

"What river is this?" Ben asked over her shoulder. She'd been so wrapped up in the view she was unaware of Cori following her across the room until she felt her presence close behind.

"The St. Lawrence River." Cori supplied the name softly as if she didn't want to break the spell that she knew had pulled Ben in as she looked out the windows. "The bank on the other side is Canada."

"You have a beautiful view." Ben kept her voice hushed as well.

"I know. It's partly what sold me on the house."

"Partly?"

"Yes, that—and the fifty acres that ensures my privacy from encroaching neighbors." She lightly touched Ben's elbow. "Come on, I'll show you the rest of the house."

Ben followed her to an open kitchen and dining area that also sported a large wall of glass. The kitchen housed gleaming black appliances in sharp contrast to the white custom cabinetry. In the center of the room an island covered in slate gray marble had two bar stools tucked under its edge.

"Does your home have these windows all along the back walls?" Ben wandered idly around the room, returning once again to the glass expanse.

"Yes. I use the downstairs level as a studio when I'm here, it gets great natural light as well." Cori's answer was matter-of-fact, but Ben detected a note of sadness in her tone.

Before she could examine it further, Cori was leading her back through the living room toward the other end of the house. Down a short hallway, she gestured to a door on the right.

"This is the guest room. You can stay in here."

"Oh, no. I don't want to be any trouble," Ben protested quickly. "I've already made reservations at the Riverview Inn."

But she followed Cori through the doorway regardless and scanned her surroundings. A queen-sized bed occupied the center of the room. The taupe walls matched one of the stripes in the predominantly navy comforter. Somehow, despite fairly plain décor, the feel of this guest retreat was warm and welcoming. Disconcertingly, her suitcase was standing on a modern rug to one side of the bed. Henry, it seemed, had already decided she was staying over.

"Ms. McClain, the Riverview is nearly forty miles away." Cori turned to face her, and suddenly Ben found the space entirely too small and her stunning interviewee entirely too close.

Intense. The word lingered in her head again. She'd never had such a visceral reaction to someone she'd just met. It was as if her mind instinctively drew in details about Cori that she didn't even realize she was noticing until she found herself wondering if Cori's skin was as soft as it looked. Or if the blond strands that brushed the back of her neck were as silky as they appeared. Irritated, she pushed the thought away, reminding herself that while Cori was physically attractive her personality probably left something to be desired.

"It's impractical to expect Henry to drive you back and forth," Cori continued in a businesslike manner that made Ben even more conscious of her own irrational response. "And it would be very costly for you to rent a vehicle that would be up to handling my drive, especially if we get that rain they've been promising. The road becomes impassable."

Cori's explanation was logical. However, Ben felt the need to argue because the slightly spicy scent that clung to the artist was making her stomach do strange things. She mumbled something vague about her schedule and the intrusion, but when Cori lifted her eyebrows quizzically she fell silent, realizing the absurdity of anything she could say.

"So, that's a yes, thank you," Cori concluded.

Ben managed a small nod. She was going to be staying in Cori Saxton's home. Lucy was going to strangle her with her bare hands for refusing the assistant offer. Bristling at being so efficiently "handled," but with no other polite alternative, Ben followed Cori back down the hall and they resumed the official tour of the house.

Cori pointed out an office with several bookcases that housed a large and obviously well-read selection of books. "Feel free to read anything you'd like," she offered with a wave of her hand toward the plush oversized chair that was tucked invitingly into the corner of the room. "My bedroom is at the other end of the hall, and, as I said before, the downstairs is mostly work space."

Making no offer to show Ben these more personal spaces, she offered, "Would you like to freshen up? Dinner will be in about an hour."

❖

The guest bathroom was on the opposite side of the hallway, directly across from the bedroom. Ben was thankful for the chance to wash her face and shed her wrinkled travel clothes. Also, to slow her breathing down. Her reaction to Cori preyed on her mind. Anyone would think she hadn't seen an attractive woman in years.

She had.

Ben argued with a voice in her head that sounded suspiciously like Lucy's, and reminded her how long it had been since she'd had a second date. Was it her fault there hadn't been any chemistry with anyone lately? She'd had her share of first dates—why, just last week she had a perfectly nice dinner with a gorgeous elementary teacher. So what if she hadn't been able to summon the interest to call the woman for a second date? She had a career to worry about and, besides, when one traveled as much as she did there wasn't much time left for dating. Ben was usually just as happy to curl up at home with a book and a glass of wine. She barely thought about how nice it would be to have someone mirroring her pose at the other end of the sofa.

Twenty minutes later, after swapping her crumpled pants and top for more casual shorts and a polo shirt, she found Cori in the kitchen wrapping sliced new potatoes and onions in foil. Having decided while she was changing that she should at least make an effort at civility, she offered, "Is there anything I can do to help?"

"You can open that wine." Cori gestured toward the bottle on the counter. She carried her foil bundles outside on the deck and placed them on the grill before returning to the kitchen. "I hope you like Cabernet Sauvignon," she said, taking a plate with two large steaks on it out of the refrigerator.

Ben nodded, glancing appreciatively at the quality vintage she'd just opened. Inhaling the rich aroma of the deep red liquid, she poured two glasses and handed one to Cori.

"Thank you." Cori registered the brush of warm fingers against hers as she accepted the glass.

The reporter was not what she had expected, even beyond the fact that she expected a man. Bennett McClain was attractive, but that alone was not reason enough to turn Cori's head. She had encountered her share of attractive women, most of them eager to get to know her better. However, something about the reporter had immediately gotten her attention—something deeper than superficial appearances. The feeling puzzled Cori. She had often felt instant attraction to a woman. Plain, unmistakable lust. But this was different. She felt oddly drawn to Bennett and despite her reluctance to do this interview, simply being in the journalist's presence inspired a nervous energy in her that she couldn't explain.

Bennett had settled herself onto a stool at the counter across from her, and as she rubbed seasoning over the steaks Cori continued to sneak surreptitious glances at her guest. When Bennett finally met her gaze, Cori was surprised to find herself sinking into eyes the hue of warm honey. She hadn't noticed the color earlier, as Bennett had been wearing sunglasses.

Realizing she was staring, she cleared her throat and spoke quickly. "How do you like your steak, Ms. McClain?"

"Medium rare. And please, call me Ben."

Cori raised an eyebrow. "Okay, Ben. And you can call me Cori. I'll be right back." With that she headed back outside to put the steaks on and check the potatoes. She was about to lower the cover back over the grill when Ben joined her on the deck.

Leaning against the railing, Ben watched Cori rearrange the steaks needlessly. She seemed a little jumpy, Ben observed—no doubt the presence of a journalist was making her a bit self-conscious.

Searching for a way to test Cori's willingness to be forthcoming with information, Ben remarked, "I just can't get over this view. I can certainly see why you would want to spend as much time here as possible."

"Ah, are we leading into the interview already?" Cori paced over to lean on the railing right next to her, their elbows almost touching.

She'd known Ben would get around to questioning her eventually, yet she still found herself resenting the obvious probing. She'd spent most of her adult life under the scrutiny of the press, sometimes intentionally seeking publicity, but often trying to avoid it. Although she never let it show, she found the attention exhausting. Even in this case, when she'd quite literally invited that unwelcome scrutiny into her home, she was already wishing she hadn't.

"That *is* what I am here for, Ms. Saxton." Ben didn't want to sound defensive, but she could hear the slight edge to her own tone. Surprised by Cori's ability to see through her, she glanced sharply at the woman standing beside her.

"It's Cori," the touchy artist said, assuming control of the conversation once more. "I thought we had already settled that. And I think the interview will keep until after dinner."

Ben produced a casual shrug. "Fine."

"I just realized I know absolutely nothing about you."

"Really?" Ben would have thought someone like Cori would have found out everything about her before agreeing to the article.

"It's very unlike me, I'll admit, but I didn't do my homework in this case. So, tell me something about yourself." Cori turned, leaning her weight on one elbow.

Ben's skin warmed under the intensity of her blue gaze. "What would you like to know?"

"The professional stuff, for starters. My agent talked me into the article and I assumed she'd checked out your previous work. But to be honest, I was so dead set against it in the beginning that—well, I was being a bit of a brat."

Ben was slightly taken aback by the offhand admission. "What changed your mind? Obviously not my impeccable reputation."

Cori let her gaze drift over the yard and across the river where she could barely make out the Canadian skyline. "I got tired of getting calls from reporters. I figured I may as well do it on my terms."

"About those terms—"

"They are nonnegotiable." Cori cut off the protest Ben had been about to offer regarding final approval of the article. "I told Gretchen—my agent, to make that clear. I'm sorry if she didn't."

"Well, that's not exactly the way I work," Ben said, unwilling to concede so early in the process.

"Then what are you doing here?"

"I had hoped to convince you to see the error of your ways." Ben was unsuccessful at masking her annoyance.

"Then I'm sorry you've wasted your time coming up here." Cori lifted her glass and carefully sipped her wine. Had she been considering backing down, the slight tremor in the hand that held her glass was a poignant reminder of the reasons why she shouldn't.

Wondering if she was bluffing, Ben briefly debated calling her on it and then decided patience was the better route in this case. Shoving the interview to the back of her mind until after dinner, as Cori had requested, she forced a polite smile and said dryly, "Then I guess I should make the most of your company before I'm thrown out."

Reading Ben's expressive face, Cori wondered if she realized how much she telegraphed. Defensiveness had jumped quickly into her eyes at Cori's insistence on retaining approval of the article. However, just as quickly she seemed to assess Cori's willingness to bend, and the sudden smoothing of her expression suggested she was not going to push her luck. When she spoke again her voice was carefully guarded.

"Professionally, I've been freelance for about five years. Before that I wrote for *Grace*."

Raising an eyebrow at the mention of the popular women's magazine, Cori pushed off the railing and moved to check the steaks. As she lifted the lid, the gentle sizzle of the cooking beef and a mouth-watering aroma drifted out.

"Why did you leave *Grace*?" she asked over her shoulder as she went back into the kitchen, leaving the door open. She returned carrying plates stacked with napkins and utensils, and one piled high with thickly cut slices of French bread. Crossing to the small table tucked in the corner of the deck, she set them down. "I thought since it's a nice evening we could eat out here."

Nodding, Ben picked up their glasses from the railing and joined her at the table. "I got tired of writing what someone else wanted me to write," she said, answering the previous question. She grinned when Cori rolled her eyes over the pointed remark. "Seriously, think about it. What if you had to paint the way someone else told you to? Could you do commissioned portraits, for example?"

Cori regarded Ben, cocking her head to the side. *She has a point.* She turned back to the grill and pulled off the steaks and the foil packages, placing them on the plates. "Have you seen my work?"

"I've seen photographs of your work."

Cori laughed. "Wow, you've really done your research for this article, haven't you?"

Ben bristled at her sarcastic tone. "Actually, I have a fairly thick file of information on you already, and there were photos of some of your paintings in there. I had somewhat short notice for this assignment, so I'm still going through it all. I thought maybe you would show me some of your work when I got here, as I'm sure that photographs don't do it justice." She purposely injected a saccharine tone in her voice, certain that Cori would see right through the false sweetness.

Chuckling at her obvious ploy, Cori extended her hand, indicating one of the chairs and when Ben settled into it, she took the one opposite. "Well, then, once you have seen my work and gotten to know me a little better, you won't have to ask if I could do commissioned work, and *portraits*, no less." She wrinkled her nose distastefully and even the word twisted as it came out of her mouth.

Ben laughed out loud. Even having seen what little of Cori's work that she had, she imagined that would be like asking Ansel Adams to photograph family portraits.

Cori lifted her glass and touched it to the rim of Ben's, ignoring the way her stomach tightened at the sound of Ben's laughter. There was something so genuine and unself-conscious in the response, it made Cori wonder where people like Ben hung out, she so seldom encountered any of them. Her pleasure was also infectious, lifting the pall that seemed to hang over her these days. Warmth spread within her as a smile transformed Ben's face. Cori's mind ran a slide show of the faces she'd used to try to chase away reality. She hadn't enjoyed any of them longer than the time it took to satisfy her lust. Yet a simple exchange and a smile from Ben was able to bring her such pleasure.

Cori took a sip of wine and then, setting her glass back down, she picked up her knife and fork and cut into the tender steak. Control. That was really what her life was all about these days. Despite the forces that threatened to upset her life, she resolved to maintain control. She controlled the terms of this interview. And she would control her reaction to Ben. She didn't need any extra reminders of just how much she had to lose by getting too close to the reporter.

They ate in companionable silence, enjoying the cool breeze that drifted up from the river. As night fell, a line of discreetly placed solar lights came on around the edge of the deck and the pool, progressing down the path to the water's edge. A nearly full moon reached across the water toward them in shimmering reflection.

Ben studied Cori as she ate. The moonlight slashed across her features, making them appear even sharper—more roguish. Ben had a sudden urge to reach across the table, to caress the shadowed indent of Cori's chin. Just as suddenly her mind clamped down around the image. *You are here to do a job. Mitch isn't paying you to fantasize about your subject.*

"So, after dinner…a tour of your studio?" Ben's words tumbled out haltingly.

Cori regarded her silently for a moment. "Okay, on one condition— tell me something else about yourself."

"Like what?"

"Well, we already covered professional. Tell me something personal." Setting down her utensils, Cori rested her elbows on the table and laced her fingers together lightly under her chin. Against her better judgment, she was curious about this reporter. Only moments ago she had vowed not to get close to Ben, but that wasn't enough to keep her from wondering about her. *On my terms. Keep it on my terms,* she reminded herself.

Ben chewed thoughtfully, considering how much she wanted to let Cori control the conversation. It was early in the process, and the illusion of control could be an effective interview tool. If Cori let down her guard, Ben's story would be that much better. And something told her that whatever was going on, she wasn't going to get to it without first gaining Cori's trust.

"Are you married? Kids?" Cori prompted when Ben remained silent. She'd noted the absence of rings on Ben's long, graceful fingers.

"No, I'm not married. And I don't have kids. I might like to someday."

"Have kids? Or get married?"

"Kids."

"Well, you're young. You've got plenty of time. How old are you, anyway?"

Ben smiled, uncertain how to take Cori's unabashed curiosity. "Didn't anyone ever tell you it's not polite to ask a woman her age?"

Cori just shrugged and lifted her glass, taking a long sip of the sweet red wine.

"I'm thirty-one."

"Do you have any siblings?" Cori asked, surprised when Ben stiffened at her words.

"You said I only had to tell you one thing about myself." Ben attempted to brush off the question but was not quite successful at blocking the image that surged into her head. Feeling the familiar ache sweeping through her body for a moment, she saw very clearly the heartbreakingly innocent face of her brother. As the ache intensified into a sharp edge of pain and loss that threatened to overwhelm her, Ben pushed it away. Settling her carefully crafted wall back into place, she cleared her throat around the lump that had formed there.

Unsure of what had caused the sudden chill, Cori filed away Ben's reaction and let the moment pass. With social grace that came from years under her mother's tutelage, she spoke quickly to cover the awkward moment.

"You're right. Just one thing. I'd offer to share something about myself, but there's probably little you don't already know or have in that thick file you referred to." Cori stood and began gathering the plates they had pushed away from them only minutes before.

"I'm sure there are a few things I don't know about you," Ben answered innocently.

She was thinking of the reason she was here, the whole purpose of the article she was supposed to be writing—Cori's disappearance. However, she realized how her words might have sounded when Cori paused and bright blue eyes blazed into hers. Her mouth went dry and she felt a flush creeping up her neck. *Gosh, Lucy would certainly get a kick out of the way I seem to be reacting to this woman.* Though she made light of her own reaction in her mind, Ben was unsettled by it and surged immediately to her feet, seeking a distraction.

"Let me help with this," she said, grabbing a serving bowl as Cori gathered the remnants of their dinner.

She tried to move past Cori without touching her, but for a split second their flesh connected when her arm slid by Cori's. Ben told herself she was imagining the electricity that seemed to arc from Cori's body to her own. But her skin refused to comply, tingling in awareness as she headed for the kitchen.

Remembering that she was only there to do a job was becoming increasingly hard after just a few hours. *Well, it doesn't help that my own body is betraying me.*

CHAPTER THREE

I guess I owe you a tour of the rest of the house, huh?" Cori took the last of the dishes from Ben and stacked them in the dishwasher, closed it, and started the cycle.

"Only if you want to. I'd love to see your work," Ben smirked, "in person. But I understand if you are private about your studio." Cori was hesitant, and Ben was still trying to gauge how much she could push and get away with.

"It's okay. Come on." Cori touched Ben's arm as she walked past her and through the living room.

"It's so peaceful. You must get a lot done when you're staying out here," Ben commented casually. She was perplexed when Cori stiffened as if the innocent comment had somehow caused offense.

"Yes, it's the ideal environment," Cori said. She usually did find herself incredibly inspired by the silence and solitude of her haven. However, this trip had been different. She hadn't actually touched a brush in almost two months. She still made a daily trek down to the studio in an attempt to ease the restlessness that came with not working. She did not feel as grounded unless she was painting. However, the panic that made her heart race, her palms sweat, and breathing erratic always chased her back up the stairs before she could lift a brush.

She knew it was a purely psychological reaction because the one time she had mentioned it to Dr. Franklin he had suggested someone she could "talk to." She had politely declined, being a firm believer that she could control her emotional and mental reactions by sheer willpower. So what if she was still working on this particular reaction? She had made progress—why, just last week she had made it all the way across the room before her chest tightened.

In truth, she had been well out of her comfort zone since the day her doctor had delivered her diagnosis. *Multiple Sclerosis.* Even thinking the words inspired a sick feeling deep in her gut and no amount of "talking" was going to alleviate it. She would simply continue to hide out until she had figured out how to handle this unexpected upheaval in her life plan. Yes, she readily admitted to herself that she was hiding, but in the face of the fear she now battled on a daily basis she felt it an acceptable reaction.

"Come," she said stiffly and led Ben to a door tucked into the corner of the foyer. She pulled it open, reaching automatically to flip the light switch just inside, and descended the stairs slowly.

As they reached the bottom, Ben was able to see a large, open room that extended almost the entire length of the house. There was a bathroom and a kitchenette at the far end, allowing the occupant the freedom to immerse herself in her workspace without having to break the spell by going back upstairs. Like the upper rooms, the northeast-facing walls were floor-to-ceiling glass; however, unlike upstairs these windows had heavy drapes that could be pulled across.

Seeing Ben pause to wait for an invitation, Cori waved toward the easel in the center of the room and the canvases leaning in rows against the walls and said, "Go ahead." She hoped Ben wouldn't notice that she didn't venture beyond the bottom of the stairs.

Needing no further encouragement, Ben wandered into the room. She traveled slowly along one wall, her eyes drifting from painting to painting, taking in the bold use of colors and sharp contrast. She'd seen similar work in photos from Cori's last show. However, she found the actual paintings much more dramatic in real life. Though she was by no means an expert, she could see why Cori had amassed such acclaim in the past few years. She was a talented artist. Her work was eye-catching and multidimensional.

As she circled toward the center of the room, Ben paused before the easel and could not prevent herself from gasping. She took a step back as a very physical reaction to the painting swept over her. *So different than the others. There is so much pain here.* The darkening shades of blue and black swirled together interrupted by violent slashes of red and white—so white it felt hot. Ben recoiled from the searing anger that swept out and over her. More curious than ever, she glanced at Cori and was surprised to find her nervously shifting from foot to foot.

Cori wanted to go back up the stairs. She felt too exposed down here and regretted allowing this stranger into her private world. *What made me want her to see this? Why do I feel like she would understand?* She'd watched Ben study the painting, golden eyes roaming over the canvas. The reactions that flew across her face were also telegraphed by her body and Cori could read every one. Shock. Puzzlement. Intrigue. It was the last piece she had touched. She'd started work on it shortly after she had arrived two months before, but had stopped suddenly in the middle of it, fighting the urge to throw it away. Since putting down her brush then, she had not returned to pick it up again.

Somehow she had known that if Ben saw it she would get a glimpse of what haunted her. Yet she'd allowed her inside the studio anyway, thinking maybe if she gave a small piece of her inner self away, the twisting pain would ease just a bit. Drawing in a shaky breath, she concentrated on being still and maintaining control, on keeping the whole story from pouring out. She willed herself not to flee into the waiting arms of this woman who stood in the center of her space. Reminding herself that Ben *was,* first and foremost, a reporter, she ruthlessly brought her emotions under control and renewed her resolve to keep her secret.

"This is…so different than the others." Ben turned to Cori, searching her face for the emotion that this canvas hinted at. She found Cori's expression closed and wondered if the shadow of pain in her eyes was mere imagination.

Cori shrugged. "I decided to go a different direction. Stretch myself a little."

"Stretch yourself?" Ben repeated skeptically. "There is obviously more to this painting than an artistic experiment."

Steeling herself against the memory of the helplessness that had inspired this piece, Cori lied, "Not really. And I think I know my own motivations as an artist."

"Come on, Cori. I only have to look at this painting to—"

"You know, for someone who has never even seen my work, you suddenly seem to be quite the expert." Cori took several quick steps into the room before lurching to a halt. She was irrationally angry. Only moments before, she had admitted to herself that she knew Ben would see the turmoil beneath the paint of this canvas, and now she was denying it.

Surprised by Cori's outburst, Ben said, "I don't have to be an expert on your work, or even on art in general, to know your painting is telling me something, even if you don't want to admit it." When Cori remained stubbornly silent, she went on, "It's striking. It makes me feel small, and...out of control."

She supposed it wasn't surprising that Cori's expression closed and whatever door had opened during their exchange was once again slammed shut. But she wished it wasn't the case. She wished she could establish enough trust that Cori would open up to her about something. Anything. Otherwise her interview was going to be sterile and superficial, like almost everything ever written about this woman.

Suddenly Ben understood that the media coverage Cori seemed to thrive on was nothing more than a coat of varnish intentionally applied to distract attention from the truths hidden beneath. Cori exposed only one dimension of herself, and she had no intention of changing that strategy for *Canvassed*. *Well, she's met her match this time.* Ben's articles weren't fluff pieces. They had depth, and she had no intention of compromising that for anyone.

Ben met Cori's uncertain gaze and could not resist challenging her. "Or have I got it all wrong, and you're just painting something to match the office décor for a corporate client?"

"I don't *do* décor." Cori shot back, anger flashing in her eyes. Here was the *Cori Saxton* Ben expected.

Unsettled by Ben's accurate appraisal of the piece, and her attitude, Cori turned away, gritting her teeth against the dull ache that had begun behind her eyes. She knew what would come next if she didn't lie down soon.

"I'm going to turn in," she said and headed for the stairs. "Feel free to linger down here as long as you'd like. Please turn off the light when you come up."

"What about my interview?" Ben blurted, caught off guard by Cori's sudden exit. She had planned to interview her that night and catch a flight out the next day.

"Isn't that what we're doing?" Cori called over her shoulder as she ascended the steps. "We can continue tomorrow."

❖

Ben leaned against the headboard of the bed with her cell phone in her hand. Flipping it open, she dialed the number from memory. Seconds later, before she could even say hello, her cousin's excited voice came over the line.

"Is she as unbelievably hot as she looks?"

Ben smiled at the envy. She could practically see Lucy's raised eyebrows and wide green eyes. "She is stunning," she admitted reluctantly, and heard an answering groan from the other end of the phone. "There's something about her that I don't think any photo could convey."

"You sound interested." Lucy could always be counted on to hear nuances that Ben wasn't even aware were in her voice.

"Of course I'm interested. It's my job to be interested," Ben said with forced casualness.

"How's the interview going?"

Here was another question that Ben was unprepared to answer. With a loud sigh, she pushed off the guest bed and paced to the window. Slipping her hand inside the seam where the curtains met, she moved one panel aside to look out. The night sky seemed clearer here than in the city, and Ben imagined that she could see every single star.

"I don't know, Luce. She doesn't even seem to want to do the interview. I'm not sure why she ever agreed. But there's definitely something she's not telling me."

"You mean like a secret?" Lucy leapt to the obvious conclusion. "Is she hiding a lover out there or something?"

"I can't quite get a read on her," Ben said, thinking out loud. She refused to examine the knot twisting in her stomach at the thought of Cori having a mysterious lover. "I expected this self-assured, womanizing—well, you know—everything you read about her in the papers. And she certainly is confident, but there's a vulnerability that I didn't expect."

Aware that she was failing to put into words the fleeting impressions she had gotten throughout the evening, Ben was at a loss for a better way to explain what she had seen. When she first noticed the faint trembling of Cori's hands as she prepared dinner, she had thought she was imagining it. But then later, as they'd argued over the terms of the article, Ben had seen something more than ego behind Cori's insistence on her approval. She'd thought for a moment it was fear, but was certain she must have been mistaken. Cori Saxton didn't come across as the type who was afraid of anything.

"Well, if anyone can get it out of her, it's you. You'll do great." Lucy could always be counted on to have complete faith in Ben.

Thanking her, Ben said good night before hanging up. Moments later, she slipped between the cool cotton sheets and closed her eyes, thoughts of Cori Saxton still drifting in her head.

❖

The full moon cast a silvery light through the windows. Though it was the middle of night, Cori didn't need to turn on any lights as she padded across the living room toward the door to her studio. She'd been dreaming that she stood in front of the easel with a brush in her hand. But when she stroked it across the canvas the paint would not leave the brush. She jerked awake filled with dread that she would never paint again. Every time she closed her eyes the dream would start all over. *It was just a dream.*

She'd climbed out of bed telling herself she just needed to get a glass of water. She just needed a minute to interrupt the loop so she could find a dreamless sleep. Drawn to the studio, she descended the stairs. Her feet stopped of their own accord as she reached the bottom. She forced herself to continue.

A palette and an assortment of brushes lay on a table next to the easel. She lifted a brush, testing its weight in her hand. Her heart raced and a fine sheen of sweat broke out on her forehead. She'd repeated this ritual before and lost her nerve every time.

This painting was more honest than anything she'd ever done. It was the turmoil, the rage, and the aching fear inside of her splashed across a canvas. She'd started it only hours after receiving the news that had turned her world upside down. Now it remained incomplete. And standing there washed in moonlight, she admitted to herself why. She was afraid if she finished it she might never find the strength to start another.

MS is progressive. I'll be able to watch my body slowly give up on me. There were too many unknowns. No one could tell her when or how the disease would move forward. But with no cure in sight, the only absolute was that it *would* move forward.

"Damn it! I just need one thing to work out right now," she muttered. Just a few months ago she had the golden touch. She couldn't have screwed things up if she'd tried. The irony of her situation wasn't lost on her.

Carbon Black. Cobalt Blue Cerulean. Titanium White. She hefted the palette in her left hand and loaded a brush with her right. She closed her eyes, and when she opened them again, she was back where she was when she started this piece; it was one of the tricks she'd always relied on, the ability to recall the inspiration almost instantaneously.

Just before the brush touched canvas she felt it. The tiniest of tremors rippled through her hand. Had she not been looking at the brush hairs she wouldn't have noticed them tremble. *Minute tasks.*

She'd been told that in the beginning she would have trouble with minute tasks. *Intention tremors.* It was a deceptive moniker. Intention, implying the tremors occurred on purpose, that she planned them. She hadn't planned a damn thing in weeks except her escape. And look how well that was working out.

Taking a deep breath, she tried one more time, fighting the quiver in her forearm until her fingers began to shake in earnest.

"Damn it!" She flung the palette against the wall. It split in two and crashed to the floor. Tears of frustration welled up in her eyes. She was losing it. And at the worst possible time.

She was still staring at the splashes of paint that were left on the stark white wall when she heard a sound behind her.

"Cori?" Ben's voice was tentative. "What's wrong?"

Cori spun around, the brush still dangling from her traitorous fingertips. Ben stood only a few feet away and she had the irrational urge to fling herself into the reporter's arms. *Reporter. She's a reporter that you've only known for a day. Get a grip, Saxton. This woman doesn't need to know that you're an emotional train wreck.*

"If there's something you need to tell me, off the record—"

"Ben, I've dealt with my fair share of reporters. If it's a good enough story, nothing is ever off the record."

Ben ignored her snide words. "Why is there paint all over your wall?"

"All right. I couldn't sleep so I thought I'd get some work done. I'm feeling a lot pressure to come up with some stuff for a new show, and I haven't been working much lately. It's making me a little nervous."

As Cori spoke, Ben bent to pick up the pieces of the palette. She crossed close enough to hand them over, and that was when she saw the moisture glistening against Cori's cheek.

"So it's work that's got you throwing things?"

Indecision flickered in Cori's eyes. For a second it seemed she would open up, then her expression hardened and Ben witnessed the lie before it reached fruition. There was more happening here than Cori was letting on. She seriously doubted that Cori usually splattered the walls with paint, and the tension in her body was evident. Ben had only known her a short time but she was certain

Cori wasn't crying over work. From the looks of things she hadn't made any progress on the painting.

"Let's just move on," Cori said dismissively. She avoided Ben's eyes, hers darting toward the stairs as if she were about to bolt.

Ben felt an unspoken pressure to move politely in that direction herself, but she resisted, asking gently, "What's the real story behind this painting?"

The compassion in Ben's eyes was nearly Cori's undoing. She wanted to tell her. It would be a relief.

"I can feel it," Ben whispered. "Fear and pain. I can feel it when I look at this painting."

She touched Cori's cheek, brushing away a tear. Cori leaned into her hand almost imperceptibly. It was enough. Ben slid her fingers into the hair that curled against the back of Cori's neck. When she drew Cori closer she was surprised to feel no resistance at all. As Cori's arms came around her waist, Ben smoothed her hands over Cori's back and shoulders. Their thighs brushed and firm breasts pressed into Ben's. She teased her fingertips down the side of Cori's neck and they drew back to stare at each other. *I could kiss her. I barely know her, but God help me, I want to.* There were mere inches between their mouths. Part of her brain insisted that she wasn't the first to fall under Cori's spell, but a growing part of her wondered what Cori's lifestyle cost her. How must it feel to exist in a world where someone always wanted something from you? How could she trust anyone?

Determined to give only what Cori needed, even if just for a moment, Ben just held her.

Chapter Four

Ben stepped out of the bedroom the next morning and slowed to a stop as she walked through the living room. She stared through the expanse of glass as the sun lifted slowly behind the horizon, sending deep reds and oranges dancing across the water toward her. She remained still, entranced as fingers of iridescent color spread over the surface. Several long moments later, startled by a clatter and a growled curse, she headed for the kitchen to find its source.

Cori stood at the counter clad only in flannel boxer shorts and a white T-shirt. She was struggling with a bottle of aspirin; the tremors that shook her hands prevented her from getting the cap off. Swearing again under her breath, she was on the verge of flinging the bottle across the room when Ben crossed to her and held out a hand. "Let me help with that."

Cori relinquished the bottle and shoved her hands behind her back, hoping Ben hadn't seen them shaking. Frustrated, she went to the refrigerator and located some orange juice, giving herself time to breathe more evenly. When she felt she had control of herself again, she set the juice on the counter next to her glass and squeezed her eyes tightly shut against the throbbing headache that had ended her restless slumber that morning.

Seconds later, her eyes flew open as Ben touched her arm. She did not resist as Ben slowly cupped her open palm and shook two pills into her hand. As the warmth of Ben's skin seeped into her own, Cori drew in a shaky breath. It wasn't so unusual for a woman to make an effort to get close to her, but what threw Cori off balance was that she wanted so much to let it happen. She stared down at the hand curled protectively around her own before returning her gaze to Ben's face. Warm amber eyes held hers for a moment, asking silently for an explanation. Cori was the first to turn away. Her skin still tingled, and she had practically melted into those eyes.

"Are you okay?" Ben sounded confused.

"I have a headache, that's all," Cori muttered, quickly pouring herself a glass of juice and downing the pills. She was still shaking, except now she was unsure how much could be attributed to the feel of Ben's palm against the back of her hand. "I'm fine."

Sensing she had somehow crossed a line, Ben changed the subject. "Did you see the sunrise? It was beautiful."

"No. I don't think a pretty sky would have helped my head," Cori replied shortly. Moving around the counter and sinking down on one of the bar stools, she rested her head in her hands, willing the pulsing pain to cease. Wanting to send a signal that they could end the small talk now, she added, "Beautiful sunrises are nothing unusual here, anyway."

Hearing the chill in Cori's voice, Ben moved away from the counter. "I'm going to shower and get dressed." *What do I care if she wants to open up to me or not. I've got a job to do. Let's not forget that.* "Is there anything else you need?" she asked from across the kitchen.

Cori spoke without lifting her head. "No. Once the aspirin kicks in, I'll be fine."

"Okay, I'll see you later, then."

"Ben." Cori's voice stopped her as she was stepping through the archway into the living room. She paused, waiting, but didn't turn around. "It's going to be a beautiful day. Come find me in a bit and we'll take a walk outside."

Nodding, Ben walked away. When she reached her bedroom, she closed the door a little too firmly and headed for the bathroom. She quickly stripped off her clothes and turned the shower on, stepping under the spray as soon as it was hot. She lingered for a moment, allowing the scalding water to ease the tightening muscles of her shoulders before reaching for the shampoo. Although she tried to focus on the mechanical process of washing her hair and cleaning her body, her mind kept replaying the events of last night.

In that brief awkward moment in the studio, she'd sensed a lowering in Cori's guard, as if Cori were inviting her to connect on some level. Now, though, it felt as if the boundaries had shifted again; Cori was obviously trying to reestablish the distance between them. Ben knew it shouldn't matter to her, but it did and she was not sure why. She had reacted immediately and intensely to Cori from the moment she first saw her and the intensity of that response wasn't fading at all. In the kitchen, when she'd seen Cori's obvious distress, it had been all Ben could do to resist the urge to cradle Cori's head and stroke her until her pain went away.

This intense desire to comfort another was something Ben had not felt since she was a child. Back then, she had wanted so badly to erase her brother's pain, and hoped desperately that somehow, if she loved him enough, he would be spared. She had been too young to understand that nothing she could do would take away the cancer destroying his young body. When he died, something inside of her had died with him.

The memory brought tears to her eyes and she turned the shower off abruptly. Minutes later, toweling herself dry in the steam-filled bathroom, she paused to stare at her reflection in the mirror over the sink. Thinking of Randall still triggered that familiar emptiness in her heart, and she knew that the lasting effects of his death were still apparent in her life, especially in the distance that remained between her and her mother. And relationships—Ben considered herself a complete failure at maintaining relationships. She was always the more distant person, always controlled, never feeling the nurturing, loving urges that she thought should be present between two people. Her feelings, it seemed, were entirely internal. She kept all of her emotions carefully buried and could not bring herself to open up to another person.

Her last relationship had survived for six months. She had cared about Heather and enjoyed spending time with her. But she could not give what Heather felt she deserved, and her mistake had been in expecting Heather to understand why.

Heather was not the first woman who had been unable to accept the emotional distance that Ben needed. Nor, Ben reasoned, would she be the last. Perhaps someday she would meet a woman who could deal with the fact that there would always be a part of herself that Ben withheld. If not, her life would simply remain as it was, which was just fine with her. She didn't need another person to feel complete. She was quite happy with her comfortably solitary life. Wasn't she?

Yet, having known Cori for only a day, Ben found she wanted to soothe the pain that she sensed within the artist. Of course, in that same amount of time, Cori had also frustrated and angered her plenty as well. In fact, she had inspired a wider range of emotions in a day than anyone had in months, and Ben found that disturbing.

Just write the article and get home. You don't need to spend any more time thinking about Cori Saxton or the way she makes you feel.

❖

When her headache eased, Cori took a hot shower and pulled on a pair of baggy khaki cargo shorts and a tight-fitting green T-shirt. Despite the discouraging events of the night before, she wandered downstairs to her studio just as she did every morning, testing.

As she approached the easel, the familiar fear and panic seized her, only this time her mind flooded with the memory of Ben's arms around her. *She caught me in a moment of weakness.* Vulnerable in the aftermath of her attempt at painting, Cori had been unable to maintain her distance as she normally did. Her utter lack of emotional control was not surprising. There seemed to be so many more moments of weakness these days, lapses she would never have allowed in the past.

Frustrated with herself, Cori turned away from the painting she suspected she would never complete and headed back up the stairs. She could regain the ground she'd lost. She just needed to reestablish her professional distance from Ben, and managing the interview as she planned would actually help with that.

Cori made her way outdoors and stretched out on a chaise on the deck, mentally rehearsing questions and answers. She was making this ordeal worse than it needed to be. All she had to do was give this journalist a printable story and say good-bye to her.

A whiff of lemon verbena floated in the morning air, and she was reminded of a faint citrus scent she'd detected the previous night, standing close to Ben. Disconcerted, Cori glanced up as the subject of her thoughts stepped through the sliding glass door. Although she wanted their association to be more businesslike, she briefly allowed her eyes, which were hidden behind dark sunglasses in deference to the lingering ache in her head, to roam over Ben's body. The journalist had dressed in navy shorts and a white and navy striped polo. Her pale skin was dusted with freckles along her forearms and over the bridge of her nose. Her hair was pulled back in a ponytail, leaving just a few stray wisps to curl over her ear and touch the back of her neck. The overall effect made her appear much younger than her thirty-one years.

Cori stood as Ben approached. "How about a walk down to the river?" she offered, determined to put last night out of her mind.

"Lead the way," Ben answered agreeably.

They took the stairs off the back of the deck and followed the stone path past the pool. Cori moved to the side, allowing room for Ben to walk next to her. Despite continued predictions of bad weather, the morning sun was holding firmly amidst the scattered clouds.

Ben felt her pale skin tightening under the warmth of the sun and glanced over at Cori, envying her smooth, even tan. She was oddly reluctant to break their comfortable silence, but she also wanted to put Cori at ease if she could, by making some harmless conversation. "Do you spend a lot of time outdoors?"

"I have recently, since I've been here."

A light breeze swept across the lawn, lifting strands of Cori's sun-bleached hair. Ben's fingers itched once again to discover whether the golden strands were as soft as they looked. Aggravated by her heightened physical awareness of Cori, she curled her hands into fists at her sides and forced her eyes away from the artist. A butterfly fluttered in front of her before settling gracefully on one of the brightly colored flowers that lined the path. They were approaching the small area in the path that had been expanded to create a small sitting area, with a stone bench surrounded by various shrubs and plants.

"Your landscaping is gorgeous," she complimented Cori.

"Henry's wife, Alma, has the green thumb. I'm not usually here enough to tend to plants." Though she enjoyed the overall effect, Cori had little interest in the names or qualities of the various types of vegetation. Landscaping had never been important to her; even when she bought the place it had been low on her list of priorities. Alma had taken it upon herself to create the gardens as a gift to Cori for making Henry feel useful again. She'd told Cori in confidence that since he retired he'd been driving her nuts hanging around the house. The several hours a week that he spent working at Cori's seemed to help.

For her part, Cori now appreciated the gardens beyond measure. Alma seemed to have sensed that she wouldn't need over-the-top bursts of color. Instead, she designed the garden for its aromatic qualities, choosing soothing lavender and varieties of evergreens as well as other fragrant flowers. During her visits, those far too rare moments of tranquility she was able to steal were often spent in the garden with a sketch pad. The rough pencil drawings of whatever flower, butterfly, or bird caught her attention would most likely never see a canvas, but she enjoyed creating them all the same. They proved a good exercise for her skills as well as an enjoyable diversion.

As they approached the dock, Cori saw Henry and gave him a wave. As usual, he was taking his maintenance job very seriously. When Cori had asked him to keep everything in working order, she had not imagined he would ruthlessly investigate every rusty nail and every inch of timber on the property; however, she was thankful that he did. Alma was happy that he found so much work for himself, and Cori was relieved that she never had to find tradesmen for every tiny repair.

"Just replacing a few boards." Henry pulled a loose plank from the steps leading to the dock and set it aside. Dropping a new one in its place, he secured it efficiently. "Alma's going to town later for groceries, do you need anything?"

"I think we're all set, Henry." Cori turned to Ben, raising an eyebrow. "Is there anything you need?"

"Oh, no. I was actually planning on leaving sometime this afternoon, assuming I get what I need from you this morning."

Cori was aware that her eyebrows had risen even farther at Ben's choice of words, her mind filling with images of just what Ben might need. Before she could form a reply Henry spoke again.

"Actually, Miss McClain, there's a storm coming this way. It looks to hit us soon. With the amount of rain they are forecasting, it wouldn't be advisable to try and get down the drive." He squinted up at Ben from where he knelt. "I don't think you'll be going anywhere until it lets up."

Ben glanced at Cori in disbelief. "But I have to—"

"We'll discuss it in a bit and decide what you should do," Cori interjected, smoothly dismissing Ben's objections. She turned her attention back to Henry. "I'll call you and let you know when it's time to pick her up."

Irritated at being brushed off, Ben was about to protest when she saw the look that passed between Cori and Henry. The older man's face was etched with concern. Cori's expression was an odd mix of a warning stare and a plea.

When Henry spoke again, his voice was low and serious. "Call me if you need anything, Cori. I mean it. Alma and I can both come over if there's a problem."

"Henry." Cori's voice held a warning tone.

Puzzled by the standoff, Ben toyed with the idea of asking if she was missing something, but she was sure that even a flippant inquiry would aggravate Cori, and she didn't need that before their interview. She decided she would interview Henry before she left, perhaps during their ride to the airport if not before. Obviously he knew something about Cori that he was not supposed to mention.

"I'll be off now." Henry stood and gave Cori another long look, absently brushing his hands against his denim-clad legs. "I'll come back and finish up here this afternoon if the storm passes quickly enough."

Cori smiled in response, making Ben far too aware of the cocky way her lips lifted, slightly higher on one side. She moved toward the end of the dock, stepping around Henry, stretching her long legs to skip the step that he had just pulled up. At the top she glanced back and offered her hand to Ben, once again enjoying the warm skin against hers as Ben allowed herself to be helped up. Cori held her hand a moment longer than necessary and Ben's fingers tingled at the contact. The heat in Cori's eyes surprised her. Her thick lashes lowered slowly and then lifted again. Unable to tear her gaze away, Ben swallowed hard as Cori's eyes darkened to a deep indigo hue. Ben realized that the arousal spreading heavily through her limbs was mirrored in those eyes.

"Ben," Cori whispered, letting her eyes drop to caress Ben's full lips. *I have to kiss her.* When she would have lowered her head, the sound of Henry's cordless screwdriver was a timely reminder that they were not alone. Shaking her head quickly, she forced her attention elsewhere, released Ben's hand, and led the way up the dock.

Ben's low whistle drew her attention as they stopped beside the Chaparral Signature 276.

"Nice." Ben's eyes ran the length of the sleek white craft. "Twenty-six feet?"

"Twenty-eight." Cori glanced with pride at the cruiser. As was true with most things she set her mind to, she had paid exquisite attention to detail, ordering the boat to her exact specifications. She had been involved in every aspect of the customizing.

Ben read aloud the words written in a flowing script across the back: "*Saxton's Pleasure.*" She raised an eyebrow, and Cori simply grinned, making Ben's heartbeat accelerate as she glimpsed the woman who had stolen so many hearts. *And she certainly knows it,* she thought cynically.

Oddly, she found she much preferred the very human woman who had held her hand and looked at her with sudden, shy desire only moments before. "Do you mind?" she asked permission before she boarded the boat.

At Cori's sweeping gesture to proceed, she stepped carefully across the expanse between the dock and the boat. She moved through the cockpit with ease, ducking as she descended into the cabin. Cori had obviously spared no expense in decorating her toy. The cabin had a double bed, a small dinette, and a well-laid-out galley and head. Tucked into one corner was a 15-inch LCD television and DVD player. When she stepped back outside, Cori was lounging in one of the seats.

"She's beautiful," Ben said. "Do we have time to take her out before the storm?"

Cori hesitated. Aware of the lingering effects of her earlier headache in the tenderness behind her eyes, she did not quite feel up to the concentration required to navigate the boat on the crowded river. She didn't want to explain why she shouldn't be driving her own boat.

Seeing her hesitation, Ben rushed to retract her words. "I'm sorry, I shouldn't have—"

"No. It's not that—" Angry with her own inadequacies, Cori's words came out harsher than she intended and she bit them off when she realized how they sounded. Having the reporter here was proving more difficult than she had anticipated and it was making her decidedly short-tempered. She took a deep breath, deciding that maybe if she stalled, she would feel up to a short jaunt soon enough. "Actually, we probably don't have time," she lied smoothly, her mask firmly back in place. "But maybe we can squeeze something in when the rain clears up."

CHAPTER FIVE

Cori served Ben an early lunch on the deck. She'd thrown together thick ham sandwiches, wedges of cheese, and fresh fruit. As they finished eating, Ben leaned back in her chair and sighed contentedly. She glanced around, once again in awe of her surroundings. She had certainly been around wealthy people before and had seen larger, more impressive homes. But something about the secluded, comfortable retreat that Cori had created drew her in. And glancing at the woman beside her, she wondered if that wasn't the purpose of it all. By all accounts, Cori had no problem finding female companionship. Was this lovely home just part of the package? Suddenly, Ben's head was filled with images of unsuspecting female victims being lured to the beautiful estate by the charming artist.

"I bet this place really impresses the women." She voiced her thoughts before she realized she had spoken aloud.

The sarcastic words made it clear exactly who Ben thought Cori was—who everyone thought she was. *Have I really given anyone any reason to think otherwise?* For years she had lived up to her reputation, enjoying the reckless life she'd grown accustomed to. And, she admitted to herself, had things not played out the way they had, she might never have had a reason to change her life. She still found all types of women attractive, but she had begun to spend more time thinking about what she wanted from her life beyond the meaningless hookups and extravagant lifestyle. She had begun to realize that she could count on one hand the number of people with whom she had ever really been genuine—to whom she had related on more than a superficial level.

For reasons she couldn't explain, Cori wanted to be truthful with Ben. She wanted to tell her that she had never brought a woman here, that it had always been her own private retreat. She wanted to tell her how her life had suddenly changed and what had made her reconsider how empty her own existence had become. By the time she had dragged herself to this upstate retreat, she could no longer remember how many women she had slept with. She had hazy memories of her most recent encounters, some involving more than one woman, but she had not been sufficiently lucid at the time to hold on to details. Looking back over the past year, Cori realized she had run the gamut from one type of woman to the next, rarely discriminating based on sexuality or marital status. She had learned early on that among the wealthy, sexuality was a flexible concept and marriage did not preclude affairs. *Straight* women often did not remain so for very long. However, they were never inclined to leave their wealthy husbands no matter how prosperous the other woman, because status was about more than just money.

Not that Cori had ever stayed with a sexual partner long enough, or been interested enough, to ask her to leave a husband or wife. She hadn't changed all that much now, she rationalized; she simply had less stamina.

A voice in her head reminded her that Ben was a journalist, and whatever direction their discussions took, the most salacious content would undoubtedly end up in print. Ben might seem to be a genuine person, but just like everyone else, she wanted something. Cori chose to give her the response she expected.

Flashing her most devastating smile, sure to make women melt, keeping her voice low and sexy, she responded to Ben's comment. "You tell me. Are you impressed?"

Ben frowned, confused by the mixed message she had detected. Cori's words and tone were seductive, but this seemed to be at odds with an underlying emotion Ben sensed beneath them. Disappointment? Cynicism? She wasn't sure.

"As a matter of fact, I am. And I become more impressed the more I learn about you." Ben answered honestly.

Everything she had discovered about this woman since she'd arrived had added unexpected facets to the enigma that was Cori Saxton. She had accepted this assignment thinking that it would be easy and that the only complication would be convincing Cori to bend her rule about approving the article. Having skimmed over the folder of information Mitchell had provided, she had thought Cori would be somewhat one-dimensional. However, there was more beneath the surface than Ben could have imagined, though she found it difficult to discern if any of it was real, or if she was merely falling for the "public persona."

Cori shifted uneasily in her chair. Most women would have responded to her flirtatious remark with something in kind, but she had a feeling she could take Ben's reply at face value. It wasn't easy to continue a seductive banter with a woman who seemed more interested in honest communication; Cori had to admit Ben had surprised her. Looking for a way out of their conversation, she glanced at the sky, which had become dark and heavy with clouds while they had their meal. The breeze was cooler now and carried on it the scent of impending rain. She was just thinking the storm was definitely coming their way when the first drop of rain hit her arm.

"It looks like we're about to be chased inside," she said, gesturing to several wet drops that now spattered the table. Standing, she began gathering up their empty plates. Ben followed her inside. "Make yourself comfortable in the living room. I'm going to straighten the kitchen and then I'll join you and we can talk about that article of yours."

❖

Ben sat at one end of the sofa with her legs curled beneath her. The file Mitchell had given her was open in her lap, and she was busy making notes in a spiral notebook. She liked to make notes rather than using a tape recorder because it forced her to capture her impressions of her subject. With a tape, it was much easier to rely on the recording to recall her interviewee's words, and she could lose the small details, for example, the change in a person's expression as they answered a particular question. Taking notes allowed her to focus on jotting down those impressions as they happened. Later, she would transfer her notes into her laptop.

She glanced up as lightning streaked across the turbulent sky. The rumble of thunder followed almost immediately. The wind whipped against the window, tearing at the trees outside, their leaves turning their backs in an effort to hold on against the onslaught. She was captivated by the power of the storm, the violence of nature—the same force that had astonished her with its beauty in the sunrise that morning.

Cori stood poised at the entrance to the living room watching as Ben seemed lost in the theatrics outside the window. Another flash of lightning flickered over Ben's face, casting her normally soft features into sharp contrast. Crossing to the sofa, Cori settled on the opposite end.

Reluctantly, Ben tore her eyes from the raging storm and turned toward her. "If this passes in a couple of hours, I can probably still get a flight today."

"I think you should wait until tomorrow and see if it lets up before you think about trying to get out of here," Cori said.

As if to punctuate her point, another bolt of lightning shot through the sky and seemed to strike the surface of the river. Ben jumped at the clap of thunder that followed. Just a couple of feet from her, the large windowpanes vibrated. Glancing nervously at the sheets of glass that were all that stood between them and the storm, Ben laughed. "How can I argue with that?"

"We're perfectly safe," Cori assured her, a little surprised by the genuine fear she glimpsed in Ben's body language. Ben closed the notebook in front of her, wondering just exactly how transparent she was. Cori seemed to know what she was thinking without very much effort.

"Is that my life story?" Cori teased, indicating the file in Ben's lap.

Ben glanced down. "I don't think it's quite that complete. It's just some background Mitchell gave me."

Cori startled her by lifting the file from her lap. Turning it around, she slowly flipped through the various candid photos, most of which were taken at this party or that bar. A large number showed

Cori with her arms around an array of beautiful women. Looking at the photos upside down, Ben was disconcerted to find she was silently comparing herself to the women in the pictures. Pushing her thoughts aside before she could examine the disappointment she felt, she lifted her gaze to Cori's face, trying to read her expression. Cori's eyebrows drew together as she studied the images. She looked detached, Ben thought, as if she were leafing through photos of some other woman, not herself.

Cori struggled to remember what she had found so appealing about those times. Certainly she'd never had a shortage of beautiful women around her, and as she looked at their faces now, flashes of encounters with them went through her mind like a slide show. But if she was being honest, she couldn't even remember most of their names; and if she was being brutally honest, she would admit most of her memories of those times were clouded in a drug-induced haze. When she was on a deadline for a show, she would stay up all night, playing hard, then use whatever chemical means necessary to stay up all day working. When the show was over and she could finally relax, she would crash, allowing herself as much rest as she could eke out before her friends started calling again to lure her to another party. There was always another party, and another girl, and looking at the pictures, she could not help but feel slightly bitter. They'd been more than willing to take everything she gave, but would any of them know how to give her what she needed most of all—someone to trust? She ached with emptiness at the thought.

"What is it?" Ben asked, struck by the sadness seeping into Cori's face. She knew she was pushing, and she told herself that it was for the sake of the article. Stifling the urge to reach out and touch the other woman, she watched with dismay as Cori shook off whatever reflection had hold of her and purposefully slid her walls back into place.

"It's nothing." She closed the file and handed it back to Ben. She'd already revealed too much of herself to this reporter, and here she was dangerously close again. She stared out the window watching the wind rip at the saplings Alma had planted that spring. She felt like one of those little trees; she stood as tall as she could, and life ripped at her and pushed against her. Sometimes it felt as if there was only so much she could bend and sway before she would break.

Feeling that she had effectively been closed out, Ben changed the subject. "Henry seems like a very nice guy."

"Yes, he is. These past years he has really been as much a family to me as my—" Cori broke off as she realized what she was saying.

"Tell me about them," Ben requested gently, attempting to ease Cori into a deeper conversation. She needed to move the interview process along but she was curious. She wanted to know more of Cori. She wanted to know what had shaped her life and made her who she was, and she wanted to watch Cori's face as she told her.

"Don't you have all that in there?" Cori pointed to the file, torn between the comfortable feeling she seemed to have, inherently, with Ben, and the reminder that everything she said was destined for a magazine article. It couldn't really hurt to talk about her family. With the public exposure they'd had for as long as she could remember, there certainly wasn't much she could say now that Ben couldn't find out with a little research.

"I want to hear it from you. It's different than reading someone else's words." Ben hesitated, thinking about just how unusual this whole assignment was turning out to be. "You intrigue me," she admitted. "And I want to get to know you. Don't think about the article, let's just have a conversation."

Cori seemed to be considering this request. Slowly she nodded. "Well, as you already no doubt know, my parents come from money—I come from money. My father worked very hard to make sure our family's wealth was secure. He values what we have, in a way that I don't think I ever really have." The words were spoken as if she was just then realizing the truth in them. Shrugging off her own seriousness, she laughed softly as she continued, "I'm an only child, and I think he always wanted a son. I guess he was pleasantly surprised when I was more interested in cars than in dolls."

"What about your mother?"

Cori's dry laugh surprised Ben. "My mother—hmm, where to start. My mother is the quintessential society wife. She is very concerned with appearances." This time Cori's tone was self-deprecating. "Needless to say, almost everything I do drives her absolutely crazy.

"When I told her I was going to be an artist, she didn't speak to me for weeks." Cori explained. "Every time a new tabloid comes out, she calls me and swears she is having a heart attack."

Ben shifted her eyes to Cori's face and found a faraway look. Cori's words dripped with sarcasm, but Ben sensed an underlying affection as she talked about her parents. A small line marred her otherwise smooth forehead and Ben wanted to reach up and rub her fingers over it. Instead she busied herself making discreet notes.

"If she only knew," Cori said softly, thinking about the secrets she had managed to keep from her mother. Changing the subject, she asked, "What about you? Are you close to your parents?"

"Not exactly," Ben answered evasively, determined not to allow the focus of their discussion to be hijacked.

"Not exactly?" Cori raised an eyebrow. She knew very little about Ben personally and, oddly, she found she was genuinely interested.

Sighing, Ben decided she would have to give a little to get a little. She'd interviewed subjects who were so eager to talk that they practically spilled their life story before she could pose a question. Cori was not going to be one of those people.

"My father left when"—Ben stumbled over her words, swallowing the explanation of her father's abandonment after her brother got sick—"when I was young. And my mother and I haven't been close in a long time." When Cori remained silent, Ben went on. "Since a very early age, I've always been very independent emotionally." She omitted the fact that most of her independence had been out of necessity.

Cori nodded. "Well, that's not necessarily a bad thing, is it? I mean being independent."

"I don't think so, but people don't really seem to understand when I sometimes seem distant."

"And by *people* you mean men." It was an obvious ploy, but Cori realized that she didn't know for sure if Ben was gay or straight. She had guessed gay, but now seemed like as good a time as any to bring it up.

Ben smiled, charmed by Cori's blatant curiosity. "Actually, by *people*, I mean women."

Meeting her eyes, Cori smiled back and as an understanding passed between them, she acknowledged it and filed it away for future consideration. She realized that as they had talked they had shifted closer to one another. Mere inches now separated them on the sofa and she had no inclination to move away.

They continued to talk while the storm raged on outside, rain pelting the windows in a steady rhythm. Ben jotted the occasional note. Mostly, though, she just listened, enjoying the soft, almost lazy cadence of Cori's voice and the casual way she gestured as she spoke. Most of what they were talking about was in the background information she already had, and therefore probably wasn't going to be in her article. She wanted a new angle, and sometime during their conversation she decided that she would stay as long as necessary in order to get it.

Eventually, she knew she was avoiding the question that would most likely interrupt the comfortable rapport they had developed. Despite their rough start, Ben sensed they had developed a tentative truce and she was reluctant to break it, but she had a job to do.

After taking a deep breath, she asked the question that would break the spell. "What are you running from?"

"I've been working nonstop for so many years. I have some big shows coming up next year. And I just needed a break," Cori answered coldly. The words sounded hollow even to her ears. Though she'd known she couldn't avoid the question indefinitely, Ben's intent gaze caught her off guard.

Ben could not believe what she was hearing. After dropping everything to come here, and breaking her own rule about approval, all because Mitchell believed there was a real story, this was what she got? *Burnout made me do it*? The excuse was so feeble, and so patently a half-truth, she asked incredulously, "I'm supposed to believe all this is nothing more than a case of burnout? You have creative exhaustion, so I have to drag myself out here and try to find something interesting to write about?" Cori bent her head to stare at her lap, avoiding eye contact. It had sounded like an okay excuse in her head, but Ben had seen right through it and she was angry, really angry. Now that she thought about it, Cori supposed Ben must be insulted on some level. Gretchen had made a big deal about her wanting to go on the record with a personal revelation about her solitude, so a serious journalist had been sent out for the scoop. But the big announcement was: *I'm tired and taking a break.*

"Why all the mystery?" Ben made the argument Mitchell had presented only days before. "If you wanted a break, you only had to say so."

"Well, there is a bit more to it than that." Cori's mouth felt like it was full of dust.

"I'm listening." Ben regarded her with a stare that was far too penetrating.

Cori's mind raced. There had to be some way she could give Ben what she needed without having to bare her soul. "I...it's difficult. It's...something personal."

Surprised by the intensity of her anger, Ben held herself in check with difficulty. "If you don't want to tell me the real reason, I'll have to accept that. Although, if that's the case, I don't know what I am doing here, because I thought it was understood that the personal reason for your withdrawal from the party circuit was to be the focus of the article."

"Why don't you just make something up? Isn't that what you reporters do?" She knew it was unfair to lump Ben in with the tabloid hounds, but she said it anyway. Ben jerked as if she'd been slapped. But when she spoke her voice was carefully controlled and carried only a trace of the anger that leapt into her eyes.

"Please don't insult my intelligence. I won't write a weak article full of excuses just for the sake of putting something out there to make your privileged life easier." Ben paused, not wanting to examine her feelings at knowing Cori was intentionally deceiving her. After all, it wasn't the first time a subject had tried to be less than truthful; they all wanted to construct their own public image. But it was the first time she had taken it personally.

She searched Cori's eyes, seeing the fear that clouded them and wishing she could understand its origin. When she spoke again her words were hard and held an edge of warning. "Don't lie to me again, Cori. I can't respect that."

Before Cori could respond, Ben stood and stormed out of the room.

"Fuck," Cori muttered under her breath, staring at Ben's retreating back.

❖

Ben's anger cooled only slightly as she closed the door to her bedroom. She paced the room, wondering why she had gotten so keyed up over Cori's evasiveness. After all, she'd certainly dealt with more difficult subjects without losing her cool. *So what is it about Cori Saxton that gets under my skin? Certainly she's attractive,* Ben admitted. *Hell, she exudes sensuality. But that doesn't mean I can't be objective. Does it? She can't be the most attractive woman I've ever been around.*

In truth, it was more than her physical appeal that drew Ben to her. It was those moments of vulnerability she sensed in Cori that fascinated her. There was something beneath the surface of Cori Saxton that had affected her profoundly. And despite her calmly delivered threat, Ben doubted she'd find the strength to walk away without knowing more.

Lifting her laptop from its case, she lowered herself onto the bed and sat cross-legged with the computer in her lap. For the next twenty minutes, she concentrated on transferring her notes to the file she had set up for the Saxton article and adding some spontaneous impressions. As she worked her mood calmed and she was able to detach from her emotions.

She was just finishing up when her cell phone interrupted. Glancing at the caller ID, she sighed heavily.

"Mitchell." She managed to keep her voice even and controlled as she greeted him.

"Ben, how is everything going up there?"

"Things are going as expected," she lied easily.

"Then I don't have to explain to you what the word 'deadline' means?"

Ben bristled at his sarcasm. "Did you or did you not tell me to do what I have to do to get you this story?"

"I did, but—"

"Then trust me, Mitchell. And try to remember the reason you sent *me* up here instead of someone else was to get a feature that will boost your circulation."

"Jesus," Mitchell grumbled. "Sorry."

"Just let me do my job," Ben said curtly. She flipped her phone closed and tossed it on the bed. "Shit," she hissed through her teeth.

CHAPTER SIX

Replaying Ben's parting words in her head, Cori wandered into the kitchen and reached for the cordless phone from the wall. When she heard the familiar voice on the other end of the line, she felt some of the tension release inside of her.

"I'm just checking in." She forced a casual tone.

"Hey, sweetie, how are you?" Gretchen's voice sounded as strained as hers.

"I'm good. How are you?"

"You know what I mean. How are you feeling?"

"A little better." Cori sighed, certain Gretchen would recognize the lie for what it was.

"It's already been over two months, Cori. Maybe you should call Dr. Franklin."

"The tremors aren't getting any worse right now." Cori could picture the frown on Gretchen's face. "I can't very well go down to see him while Ben is here, maybe after she leaves." On some level she knew that Gretchen's concern was not baseless. This particular relapse had lasted longer than the previous one.

"Ben?"

"I'm sorry, the reporter, Bennett McClain."

"You haven't told her the truth, have you?" Gretchen's concern was evident.

"Not yet."

"*Not yet?* Jesus, Cori, she's a reporter. Everything you say will go straight into Mitchell Gardner's damn magazine." Gretchen raised her voice. "I thought the plan was to tell him—*her* the exhaustion story, drop a few hints about rehab, and get rid of her fast."

"Do you think I need you to tell me that?" Cori shot back, matching her tone.

"I'm sorry, I'm just worried about you."

"I know."

"Are you taking your meds?"

"Yes, but you know how they make me feel." More than once, Gretchen had held a wet cloth to her head while she lay shaking and sweating in bed. Gretchen had also witnessed the severe headaches that were a side effect of the drugs.

"I know. But Dr. Franklin said that should lessen. You've only been on the Betaseron for a couple of months." Cori's doctor had prescribed the medication—a drug in the family of interferons, which are intended to assist in the regulation of the immune system—in an effort to reduce the frequency and severity of her relapses. The side effects she had been experiencing were expected to lessen over time as her body acclimated to the drug.

"I know."

Cori surged to her feet, turning as she did and stopping short when she came face-to-face with Ben hovering near the kitchen threshold. *Shit, how long has she been standing there?* Cori frantically searched her mind to recall her side of the conversation thus far, wondering if she'd given anything away.

"Cori?" Gretchen's voice startled her. She hadn't realized that she still held the phone to her ear. Unaware of what she was saying, she quickly mumbled an excuse and hung up, her eyes never leaving Ben's face.

"I'm sorry. I didn't mean to intrude." Ben had been about to back out of the room when Cori caught her standing there. She hadn't meant to eavesdrop, but when she heard Cori's raised voice and obvious frustration, she had lingered for a moment.

Cori stared at her for a minute longer and then waved away the apology. "It's okay. We were just having a professional difference of opinion."

Cori moved to return the phone to the cradle at the same time as

Ben stepped into the room. They passed within inches of each other, and Cori's stomach tightened in reaction to the citrus scent drifting from Ben. *Shampoo.* Cori recognized the brand that she kept stocked in her guest bathroom. *Get a grip, Saxton, it's just shampoo.*

Still unsteady from her conversation with Gretchen, and unsure just how much Ben had overheard, Cori hastily excused herself and slipped from the kitchen. In the past, her studio had always felt like a refuge. Now, as she went down the stairs, apprehension coiled inside of her with every step. She'd decided to increase the frequency of her visits to the studio with the intention of at least dulling the sharp edges of her reaction.

When she reached the bottom of the stairs, she stared unseeingly across the room. Stalling, she let her mind wander back over her earlier conversation with Ben. She could no longer remember why she had agreed to the interview thinking that she could convince an astute journalist that something severe enough to send her fleeing her active social life was as simple as professional fatigue. But as she considered it, Cori realized that she hadn't really had the energy for that life for some time. She had been growing bored with the same faces and the constant stream of women who were only interested in her money and the attention they gained by being seen with her and had continued with her routine mostly out of habit.

Cori almost laughed at herself. Apparently a couple of days with a woman like Ben was enough to convince her that she had been seeking out the wrong women. *A woman like Ben?* Cori was not even sure she knew what that meant. There seemed to be so much about Ben she didn't know, such as what caused the sadness in her eyes when she talked about her family. They'd barely interacted on anything more than a professional level, but there were things about Ben that she just seemed to be able to sense, like her underlying strength, honesty, and straightforwardness.

Ben's warning as she'd left the living room earlier echoed in her mind. *Don't lie to me again, Cori. I can't respect that.* Why was gaining Ben's respect suddenly so important?

She took several hesitant steps toward the canvas in the center of the room. Her gaze traced the vibrant lines of the painting, and she recalled the numbing fear and hurt that tore at her every time she put a brush to this canvas. *This is what Ben wants. She wants me to show her where this came from.*

Could she do it? Could she tell Ben the whole story? She found the idea decidedly less frightening than she might have thought. But Gretchen was right—if she did so, she did it with the knowledge that Ben would print it. If she told her, it wouldn't be fair to ask her not to.

❖

Ben found Henry by the river again, working to repair portions of the dock. As her footsteps sounded on the wooden planks, he spared her only a glance before returning to work.

"That storm passed through quickly," she commented as she approached.

"It certainly did, Ms. McClain," he said between fastening boards. "It's going to be a nice afternoon."

"Will it disturb you if I sit for a while?" Ben waited until he gestured for her to go ahead, then sat down, dangling her legs over the edge of the dock. "How long have you known Cori?" she asked as Henry continued to work.

"About five years."

"Does she spend much time here?"

He paused in his work. Setting down his hammer, he regarded her silently for a moment before he answered. "Ms. McClain, with all due respect, aren't you here to interview Cori?"

"Yes, I am, Mr. Rollins. But it's not unusual for me to interview friends and family for a celebrity feature like this. Besides, she hasn't exactly been an open book." She didn't pretend innocence; he knew she was fishing for information.

"Well, then, I don't know what you hope I can tell you. But you should be asking her instead of me," he replied resolutely.

"If you are worried about your job, I can guarantee you complete anonymity with regard to anything you tell me," Ben offered confidently. She had experienced token resistance before. But she'd also found that the wealthier a subject was, the less loyal their employees turned out to be. The promise of confidentiality often elicited the information she needed. However, there was a line between assuring a source remained anonymous and offering to pay for information. Regardless of what Cori seemed to think of her, Ben would never cross that line; despite the attractive rates, she did not work for tabloids.

Instead of being insulted by her assumption about his loyalty, Henry simply chuckled at her impertinence. "Ask Cori," he repeated.

"Ask Cori what?"

Ben jumped at the words spoken so closely behind her. She hadn't heard Cori approaching them and wondered how much she had heard. "Nothing," she mumbled.

Henry stood and gathered his tools. "I've got to get home. The grandkids are due to visit this evening. I'll see you later, Cori."

"What did you get him so fired up about?" Cori joked after he left.

Ben tilted her head back to look up at Cori. "I have a feeling he doesn't get fired up about anything."

Feeling at a disadvantage, she scrambled to her feet, only to realize that she was face-to-face with Cori, entirely too close for comfort. She immediately stepped back and was startled when Cori firmly grasped her waist and pulled her closer. Ben gripped Cori's shoulders automatically in an effort to steady herself.

"You don't have much room back there." Cori glanced down at their feet.

Ben followed her gaze to find that she stood only inches from the edge of the dock and would most likely have stepped backward right off it. Her words of gratitude died in her throat as Cori's indigo eyes moved languorously over her face. She could practically feel their unhurried caress.

"Ben," Cori whispered. Her skin burned through her shirt where Ben's hands rested on her shoulders. A pulse point jumped rapidly at Ben's throat, and for a moment, Cori allowed herself to wonder how that skin would feel beneath her lips. Would it be slightly salty and sun-warmed?

"Yes." Ben's eyes were riveted on Cori's lips. She could lean just a few inches and touch them with her own.

Cori looked past Ben's shoulder toward the river. "We have company." Reluctantly dropping her hands, she stepped away. As soon as she had gained some distance, she mentally kicked herself. What happened to keeping things on a professional footing? Her resolve seemed to die as soon as they were within a few feet of each other.

Ben turned to see a flashy white and yellow boat approaching the dock. As it neared, the two occupants waved enthusiastically.

"Hey, Saxton." The shorter one greeted Cori with a wide grin as they pulled alongside the dock. Dark sunglasses screened her eyes, and her short blond hair stood on end.

"Hello, ladies," Cori returned the greeting.

"How about joining us for a little cruise?" the other woman called out. "Grab your swimsuits."

"We'll be right back," Cori replied, evidently taking Ben's agreement for granted.

"I didn't bring a swimsuit," Ben said quietly as Cori steered her toward the house.

Cori's eyes raked over Ben from head to toe. "I'm sure I have something that will fit you."

CHAPTER SEVEN

Cori handed over the small cooler she had stuffed with drinks and snacks, then stepped onto the boat. Holding out her hand, she helped Ben on board, ignoring the swift stab of pleasure that she was coming to expect whenever they touched.

Ben settled into the bench seat on the side of the cockpit, and Cori dropped down beside her. The blonde slowly backed the boat away from the dock, turning it downriver.

"Guys, this is Ben, she's here to do a story on me for *Canvassed*. Ben, our driver over there is Janet, and," Cori gestured toward the petite redhead who sat to their left, "this is Karen."

Ben smiled at them both.

"Nice to meet you, Ben," Janet said with a friendly grin. "Hey, Saxton, how've you been?"

"I've been good," Cori lied.

"We haven't seen you on the water lately."

"I've been busy. Working." Another lie.

They anchored in a small inlet away from the swifter currents of the river and snacked on sandwiches, potato chips, and chocolate chip cookies. Cori passed out bottles of cold beer and soda. As they ate, Ben made mental notes while Cori and Janet took turns trading stories. They had known each other since Cori bought the house. Janet and Karen had been seeing each other for two years and were now living together.

"Janet has always been the more outgoing of the two of us," Cori explained, turning to Ben.

"Yeah, right. Remember that time we drove up to Montreal, and you—"

"Oh, no, no, you can't tell that story," Cori interrupted vehemently.

"What was that woman's name? Kristen? Kaitlyn? Something like that." Janet tilted her head back, fingertip to her chin, as if struggling to recall the details. She grinned as Cori shot across the small expanse of the boat and put a hand playfully over her mouth.

"Please, Janet, I'm begging. Don't tell that story. Is that really the story you want my mother reading about in Ben's article?"

Laughing, Janet pulled her head free from Cori's grasp. "Come on, Saxton, I'm not buying that. Your mother has heard a lot worse about you."

Giving up, Cori resumed her perch beside Ben and turned imploring eyes on her. "Don't believe a word she says." She lowered her voice, whispering loudly enough for Janet to hear. "She has a very rich fantasy life." She ducked as a cookie flew at her head.

"Okay, you big baby," Janet relented. "Come on, let's go swimming." She quickly stripped off her shorts and T-shirt and jumped in the cool water.

Standing, Cori pulled her tank top over her head, revealing a lean, tight torso clad only in a light blue bikini top. Ben stared as Cori dropped her shorts and approached the edge of the boat. Seemingly unaware of the effect she was having on Ben, Cori slipped over the edge, following her friend into the water.

Swallowing hard, Ben tore her eyes away from the spot where Cori had just been. In the space of a few moments, the image of Cori's nearly perfect body was burned behind her eyes.

"Pretty impressive, huh?" Karen slid onto the seat beside her.

"Uh—" Ben flushed.

Karen laughed at Ben's obvious discomfort at being caught ogling Cori. "She's gotten thinner since the last time I saw her, though," she remarked innocently.

Ben flashed on the image of Cori just before she slid into the water. Her abdomen was tight and flat, and her tanned skin stretched tautly over her ribs. Firm breasts and strong shoulders and arms were no doubt made so by hours spent standing behind an easel.

Suddenly Ben was struck with an overwhelming urge to watch Cori paint—to see whether her motions were smooth and measured or if they were frantic, as if she was trying desperately to capture an image before it fled her mind.

Hearing Karen clear her throat beside her, Ben flushed deeper. "Sorry," she mumbled.

"Girl, please, if I wasn't happily married, you'd have some competition," Karen teased.

"Oh, no," Ben rushed to correct her. "It's not like that."

"Uh-huh, sure." Aware of Ben's growing embarrassment, Karen relented. However, she didn't buy the denials for a second. She had seen the way Ben looked at Cori. And from the glances she had seen her friend returning when she thought no one noticed, Karen was willing to bet that the feeling was mutual. Even if neither of them knew it yet, they definitely set sparks off each other.

"Are you enjoying yourself?" Cori turned her head lazily to the side to study Ben. The journalist's cheeks and nose were tinged pink from exposure to the late morning sun. A strand of hair, still wet from their swim, clung to her cheek, and Cori's fingers itched to brush it back but she was not sure that the caress would be welcome.

"I am. Very much." Ben was ridiculously aware of Cori stretched out on the seat beside her.

"Good. I'm glad." Cori's voice was low, almost hypnotic. She lifted her legs one at a time and extended them, flexing each foot.

"Your friends are great," Ben said distractedly. Her eyes refused to leave the firmly muscled limbs. She hoped her dark glasses hid her preoccupation.

Cori studied Ben out of the corner of her eye. The borrowed one-piece black swimsuit didn't fit perfectly, but it still managed to show off her curves nicely. When Ben suddenly leaned forward to get another beer from the cooler, Cori caught sight of a tattoo peeking out from under the edge of the strap of the suit. Reaching out, she pushed the fabric aside. Several small black oriental symbols ran vertically down Ben's shoulder blade.

"I hadn't figured you for the tattoo type," she remarked. "What does it mean?"

Ben froze as Cori's fingers brushed lightly over the symbols. When she spoke, she didn't look at Cori. "Pain. Courage. Love."

"That's beautiful." Cori was intrigued. No one chose a tattoo like that without a reason. *Pain. Courage. Love.* She wondered what lay behind the symbol.

"It's a reminder of something I lost," Ben said so quietly Cori almost didn't hear her.

When she didn't volunteer anything more, Cori didn't press, but she continued to stroke her shoulder.

Giving in to a moment of weakness, Ben leaned into the caress. Cori's fingers moved higher, tracing along the top of her shoulder and slipping beneath her hair to the back of her neck. Ben shivered. When Cori's fingers twined in her hair and tugged gently, Ben moved closer, leaning against her.

The hypnotic motion of the boat rocking gently in the water combined with the rhythmic feel of Cori's fingers sifting through her hair had Ben's eyes closing in lethargic surrender. As they had come out of the water earlier, Cori had pulled her shorts back on but had left her T-shirt off. Now the sun-warmed skin of Cori's long legs and upper body pressed against the length of Ben's. A contented sigh escaped her.

Cori too had fallen under the spell of their surroundings. Somewhere in the back of her mind she registered the quiet conversation and splashing of her friends outside the boat. But more present was the feel of silky strands of hair that slipped through her fingers, the comfort of Ben's weight against her, and Ben's soft, even breathing. She glanced at Ben's face, taking in her closed eyes and peaceful expression. Touching Ben felt so natural and right that the desire to kiss her stole into Cori's heart before she could stop it. *Don't! It wouldn't be fair to her.*

At the very moment that Cori was desperately trying to talk herself out of the kiss she ached for, Ben opened her eyes and Cori suddenly found herself lost in irises the color of fine aged whiskey.

Startled to find Cori watching her, Ben froze. She felt self-conscious but also intrigued. The expression in Cori's eyes was unmistakable. Her body quickened at the lust burning there, and without thinking, Ben closed the distance between them. She felt Cori stiffen as their lips met. Within seconds, however, their bodies melted together. Ben lifted her hands to frame Cori's face, her thumbs stroking over her jaw. Cori's fingers tangled in the back of Ben's hair and her stomach tightened. Ben's kiss was tentative, but when Cori responded, she became bolder, running her tongue gently over Cori's lower lip. Her arms slipped around Cori's neck and as Cori's tongue slid against hers, Ben leaned back, drawing Cori with her. *Christ, this feels so perfect.* Cori's body half covered hers.

A clunking sound slid through the fog of arousal clouding Cori's brain, and she drew back just as Janet's head appeared over the side of the boat.

"I'm sorry—" Cori began automatically.

"Please, don't apologize. I'm the one who kissed you," Ben said.

"But—"

"Don't." Ben looked away, her face flushed.

Cori stifled a groan. *I shouldn't have let you kiss me. How will I ever stay away from you now?*

CHAPTER EIGHT

Ben's steps slowed as she walked into the living room after having showered and changed. Cori was curled up at one end of the sofa, a bottle of beer cradled between her hands. When Ben entered, she glanced up, then shifted her eyes away. Uncomfortable, Ben considered retreat, but she decided they would have to deal with what had happened eventually. Settling carefully on the other end of the sofa, she took a deep breath.

"Listen, about what happened—earlier—um, on the boat."

"It's not necessary." Without looking up, Cori dismissed whatever Ben was about to say with a wave of her hand.

"I need to—"

"Ben, it's not necessary." Cori cut her off more sharply this time, finally looking at her. It was a mistake. Ben's damp hair and flushed skin from her recent shower lent her a vulnerability that rattled Cori.

"I haven't acted so unprofessionally—well, ever." Pushing off the sofa, Ben began pacing the length of the room. "I mean, to cross a line like that with an interviewee, it's—it's crazy."

"Do you always do that?" Cori leaned forward, bracing her elbows on her knees, and watched Ben thoughtfully. Why should she suddenly find it so incredibly cute that Ben paced when she was nervous?

Ben stopped, turning to look at her. "Do what?"

"That." Cori gestured with her hand. "The pacing."

"Um, yes. Yes, I guess I do."

"Interesting." And with that, Cori stood and moved to intercept her, forcing Ben to come to a halt in front of her. Her eyes lingered on Ben's face, then swept down to the pulse at the side of her throat. Fighting the urge to touch that point and feel the blood race beneath her fingers, Cori curled her hands into fists at her sides. "Now, I *do* need to clear up one thing."

"What?" Ben allowed herself to meet Cori's eyes and was instantly lost in the varying shades of blue in their depths. She had given herself a firm lecture while showering and had come away with the resolve that she would apologize and set them back on a professional course. And yet for all of her good intentions, she had lost control of the situation as soon as Cori looked at her.

"You don't have all the responsibility here," Cori said firmly. "If you think about it, I'm sure you will recall that I participated as well."

Ben did think about it. She had done nothing *but* think about the sensation of kissing Cori, of holding her. She thought about it now, standing so close that her body came to life. Stunned by the all too vivid memory of Cori's tongue sliding against hers, Ben whispered, "I can still taste you."

Cori gasped as a sharp stab of arousal shot through her. "Christ, Ben, you can't say things like that."

Between their close proximity and Ben's softly rasped words, she was instantly wet and ready. Cori stepped back, putting distance between them. *How did she turn the tables on me so quickly? One minute I'm in control, and then with a few words I'm all fired up and melting inside.*

Ben too was grateful for the distance Cori reestablished. The words had escaped before she could stop them, and now there was no way to call them back. She had barely managed to avoid cringing as they echoed in her head. Ben retreated until her back came solidly into contact with the wall. "I'm sorry."

"Please, stop apologizing to me." Cori's eyes were impossibly dark and her body visibly tense.

Ben kept her distance, struggling to clear her head. "We need some kind of truce here. I've got an article to write, and I need to be as objective as I can. We have to get this interview done." She refused to think about the feelings Cori stirred in her. They had absolutely nothing to do with her job. So what if she was having a physical reaction to the woman? She was a grown woman; surely she could control her urges. She had an obligation to Mitchell and she intended to fulfill it.

Lost in her own body's surging desire, Cori missed the conflicting emotions that flickered across Ben's face. When she'd read her so easily before, she now only heard the words. Ben had a job to do, and that was all that mattered to her. *She's here to write an article, why should she care about you, Saxton? She doesn't even know you.*

"Of course, your article." Frustrated, Cori forced her thoughts back to their conversation. Floundering momentarily, she took a defensive tack. "You just do your job, and I'll try not to resent it."

"Damn it, Cori, why do we have to do this? You agreed to this article, and yet every time we start to make progress, you get evasive." Her frustration rising to match Cori's, Ben met Cori's eyes.

Once again lost in Ben's golden gaze, Cori blurted out the first thing that came to mind. "It's just not that easy having your privacy invaded. I mean, I've put my whole life on hold to have you here."

"Is that what this is about?" Ben paused, studying Cori, trying to assess the degree of truth in her words. "Is that really why I haven't seen you working since I've been here? Am I disturbing your work?"

Cori debated her answer. Ben had a way of asking a question as if she really cared about the response. For reasons she could not explain, Cori wanted to answer—honestly. However, the fear that they were spiraling dangerously toward the truth had her censoring herself. She was not quite ready to change the way Ben looked at her.

"No. I haven't worked in some time," she admitted.

"Why?"

"Will you accept—I just haven't been inspired?"

Ben regarded her suspiciously. "If it's the truth."

"It's part of the truth."

Cori had never realized how much a part of her identity her work was. The knowledge that she might someday be unable to continue was so painful that she had simply stopped. Yet doing so had left her so completely unsure of herself. Gone was the confident, almost arrogant, woman. In her place was a lost soul, who was now questioning what, if anything, she had to offer. Was she that afraid of losing her ability to paint? She had never realized before just how much being an artist had defined her. She knew where she stood in that world.

"I need to hear the rest of that truth," Ben said quietly.

Cori sighed. "Soon. Tonight, I promise."

❖

Hearing a faint buzzing noise, Ben looked up from where she was slicing tomatoes. She had offered to make the salad for dinner as a peace offering and in an attempt to occupy her mind. She had been taken aback by the defeat in Cori's voice as she promised her the truth. *Soon. Tonight.* The buzzing noise persisted, Cori's cell phone vibrated against the counter.

"Cori," she called out.

Laying down the knife, she picked up a towel and wiped her hands as she took a few steps toward the living room where she had last seen her.

"Cori!" There was no reply and the room was empty.

Picking up the phone and glancing at the display, she headed through the living room and down the hallway toward Cori's bedroom. The door was slightly ajar and she peered hesitantly through the gap as she knocked.

"Cori, I—" Ben stopped short. Cori was sitting on the bed with a syringe in her hand.

Cori's hand froze in midair. She was perched on the edge of the bed with her shorts pushed up high on her leg, having just finished administering the injection in the middle of her thigh.

"What are you doing?" The phone call forgotten, Ben stared, trying to make sense of what she was seeing.

Suppressing the urge to jump up, Cori said, "It's not what it looks like."

"It's not?" Ben's eyes remained glued to her hand. "'Cause it kind of looks like you're shooting up."

Cori carefully set the syringe on the nightstand. "This isn't how I wanted you to find out."

"Find out what?" Ben's voice rose, though Cori's was so quiet she had to strain to hear her. "Drugs? Is that what all this about?"

Ben retreated until her back was against the door frame. Her mind raced and her heart twisted. This was not at all what she had begun to expect. She didn't want to believe that Cori had a drug problem, but the evidence seemed to be staring her in the face. The exile must be a kind of rehab. Ben almost choked. Why would Cori try to hide that? These days rehab was virtually a badge of honor for most celebrities, almost a get-out-of-jail card.

Cori palmed one of two small bottles from the nightstand. Her eyes raced over Ben's face. Everything was about to change and she wanted to delay the inevitable as long as possible. She looked pointedly at the phone in Ben's hand.

"Uh—your phone was ringing." Ben glanced down at the now inactive device. "It was Gretchen and I thought it might be important, so I…" Her voice trailed off as she realized the ridiculousness of the explanation.

Neither woman moved for several long seconds. Then Cori got off the bed and crossed to the door. She slowly held out her hand, opening it to reveal the vial resting in her palm.

Ben took the bottle and read the label. "Betaseron. What is this?" She didn't recognize the name of the medication, but the pharmacy label bearing Cori's name indicated that illicit drugs were not the problem.

"It's supposed to decrease the frequency of my relapses." Ben looked up sharply. Cori's next words were delivered quickly as if she had to get them out before she changed her mind. "I have multiple sclerosis."

"Jesus, Cori," Ben whispered. She leaned weakly against the wall, searching Cori's face for some sign that she had misheard.

What she found instead was evidence of fatigue. Shadows darkened the tender skin under her eyes. Her face seemed to have become thinner, just in the short time Ben had known her. Ben suddenly had the urge to lay her palm against the hollow below Cori's cheekbones. Numbly, she handed the medication back to her. "I don't—I don't know what…"

Forcing herself to remain calm, Cori took Ben's hand, persisting when she felt slight resistance, and twined their fingers together. She drew her into the room, pulling her down to sit next to her on the edge of the bed. She had put off Ben's finding out about her illness for as long as she could. Telling Ben meant it would be in her article, but more than that it meant Ben would look at her and see weakness, and for reasons she did not wish to explore that bothered Cori more.

"I'm sorry, I don't know that much about multiple sclerosis," Ben said numbly, staring at Cori and trying to absorb what she had just heard. Her mind and body warred with opposing instincts, to flee or to draw Cori close and hold her.

Cori took a deep breath, but still her voice was shaky when she spoke, "It affects everyone differently. In my particular case, so far it seems to be primarily affecting my arms and hands." Saying the words made them feel so real. Cori's hand unconsciously tightened around Ben's, searching for an anchor as her world swam around her.

"How bad is it?" Ben squeezed back. Her voice was steadier than her feelings, her professional side taking over.

"It's not too bad yet. But—" Cori's throat closed over the remainder of her words.

"Tell me," Ben implored.

When Cori spoke, her voice was distant, her eyes unfocused as she recounted the story of her diagnosis. For over a year, she had chalked up the sporadic episodes of blurred vision and overall fatigue to too much work and not enough rest. She had even managed to convince herself that the loss of feeling and control in her hands was minor. After the third prolonged occurrence, when the numbness spread up her forearm, she had sought the advice of her physician, who eventually referred her to a neurologist. Upon completing a battery of tests she was summoned to Dr. Franklin's office.

He didn't sugarcoat it, and for that Cori was grateful. After the first sharp punch of pain at his words, her distress had faded into numbness as she sank down on the edge of his sofa.

Her fingers still entwined with Cori's, Ben watched Cori's face. Her dark eyes were unreadable, her expression tight and the muscles of her jaw bunched. Still reeling from the revelation, she struggled to keep up as Cori continued talking.

Upon leaving Dr. Franklin's office, Cori had immediately gone home and set about researching her condition. With each word she read, her heart sank further. There was plenty of information to be found on the Internet regarding promising treatments and various medications. However, in Cori's state of mind, she had seen only the dim prognosis. *Progressive.* What had begun as an inconvenience would, with all certainty, someday become a serious disability.

"When I'm symptomatic, I have difficulty with tasks that require dexterity," she said suddenly. Pulling her hand free, she crossed the room to stare out the window.

"Like the aspirin bottle?" Ben asked, standing and joining her at the window.

Cori nodded. "They're called intention tremors. Simplified, it means that while at rest, my hands don't usually shake, but the more minute the task, and the harder I try, the worse the tremors become."

"Is—is there anything they can do?" Unable to keep from touching her, Ben brushed her hand down Cori's arm.

"There are drugs, like Betaseron, that can help with the relapses. There are also some steroids that will treat specific symptoms. But there's no cure. My symptoms are really not that bad right now. I've just got to be aware of a few limitations. Over the years, though, they will worsen." The words jerked to a halt as she said them aloud.

"How bad?" Ben asked.

Cori searched Ben's eyes for traces of pity but she found only concern and something deeper. "There's really no way to tell how fast it will progress or to what degree I'll be incapacitated." She forced herself to state the facts as bluntly as she could, testing her own reaction to the words as well as Ben's.

Incapacitated. Ben cringed.

❖

"Do you think you have enough for your article?" Cori propped her feet up on the coffee table in front of her. They had returned to the living room and settled on the sofa to talk. Cori had filled Ben in on the basics of MS, explaining that it was characterized by lesions that formed in the nerve fibers of the central nervous system. The varying possible locations for these lesions accounted for the wide variety of symptoms MS could present.

Forcing herself to appear calm, Cori talked more in depth about her own experiences. She described the tests she had endured and her feelings of uncertainty. While she talked, it was as if she was watching from outside herself—hearing someone else's voice. She just kept thinking that the deed was done. Soon, her own personal battle would be made very public, put on paper for anyone to read, and put there by Ben's hand.

"I think so. I'll probably do some basic research on MS—pull some statistics, that sort of thing." Ben's gaze lingered on Cori's hands, which she had been rhythmically clenching and unclenching in what Ben had figured out was a nervous gesture.

"Cori, I understand why this article is difficult for you, this is a very private thing," Ben began tentatively. "But I get the feeling there's more to it than that."

Cori stared at her for a moment, struggling to put her own thoughts in order. She'd known the MS was not something she would be able to hide forever without seriously altering her lifestyle. And the fact that she had done just that and had drawn more attention to herself did not escape her notice. So maybe she could regain a sense of control by managing the manner in which her diagnosis was disseminated. What was important now was that she find a way to make Ben understand what these past few months had been like for her.

"Come with me," Cori said, suddenly surging to her feet.

Without waiting to see if Ben was following, she strode through the living room and toward the door to her studio. She remained silent as they descended the stairs. Fighting the panic that rose in her throat, Cori moved directly to the center of the room to stand in front of the easel.

"See that slash of white?" With an angry flick of the wrist, Cori indicated a line in the lower left portion of the canvas. "That bend in the middle was unintentional."

"I wouldn't have known that if you didn't tell me," Ben replied without thinking. She knew it was wrong the moment she said it, but her first instinct had been to ease Cori's worry. Instead, Cori stiffened and turned away. Too late, Ben understood. Painting was not an exact science and often a piece did not come out exactly as it had been conceived. But this error was symbolic of Cori's loss of control.

"You don't understand." Every time she looked at this canvas it was as if she could actually feel the disease inside her, like a sinister shadow growing until someday it would be stronger than she was. And somehow the knowledge that Ben truly didn't understand why that tiny imperfection of paint was a glaring reminder of her illness hurt more than she wanted to admit.

"I do. I do understand. But I don't know why you think this has to be the end of your work. There is so much more you could do."

"Like what?" It was a rhetorical question, really. As she stared at the vivid reminder of her impending failure on the canvas in front of her, Cori was past the point of listening seriously to Ben's suggestion.

"You're a gifted artist. You could teach."

"Haven't you ever heard the expression—'those who can, do'…" She trailed off, leaving the rest unspoken. *Those who can't, teach.*

"You don't believe that." Ben took a tentative step forward but Cori was already drawing away.

"I'll make arrangements for Henry to drive you to the airport first thing in the morning," Cori said quietly as she crossed the room and slid open the door to the patio.

"Where are you going?"

"For a walk." And with that she disappeared through the door. Ben moved to the window and watched as Cori made her way down the path and out onto the dock. Her eyes remained on Cori until she boarded the boat and disappeared belowdecks.

Chapter Nine

Cori awoke to the insistent ring of the telephone. As she rolled over a little too quickly for the throbbing in her head, her arm shot out in a desperate effort to stop the noise. She finally managed to fumble the phone off the cradle and rasped a greeting into it.

"Are you still sleeping?" Gretchen's chipper voice grated across her nerves.

"Not anymore," Cori grumbled.

"Do you know what time it is?"

"Don't start." Cori glanced at the clock—nearly noon.

"The new issue of *Canvassed* came out today," Gretchen went on, "I'm already getting calls from the press."

"Vultures," Cori muttered, rolling out of bed and stumbling toward the bathroom.

Hitting the button for speakerphone, she set the phone on the counter next to the sink and bent over to splash some water on her face. Dimly aware of Gretchen talking, she picked up the phone and made the appropriate sounds to let Gretchen know she was still listening. Barefoot and clad in boxer shorts and tank top, she padded to the kitchen and poured herself a glass of juice.

Glancing at the counter, she caught sight of the note Ben had left for her. It had been two weeks since Ben had left. Cori had spent that night on the boat, though the normally soothing sway of the waves didn't calm her and she had slept fitfully. She had not returned to the house that next morning to see Ben off, trusting Henry to pick her up on time. Instead, she waited until she was sure Ben was gone before slipping through the back door into the kitchen. That was when she found the note. The folded piece of paper read, *Thanks for your hospitality. Best wishes, Ben.* And with it, Ben had left one of her business cards. Every time Cori passed through the kitchen, she paused to read it.

"Cori, are you listening to me?" Gretchen's raised voice startled her.

"What? Uh, yeah," she answered distractedly.

"What did I say?" Gretchen challenged.

"Okay, you got me. I'm sorry. But I have a lot on my mind right now." Cori picked up the business card. The linen textured card felt thick between her fingers. Ben's face floated into her head as she rubbed her fingertips over the slightly raised script. Hard as she tried she could not keep from remembering the heavy-lidded expression on Ben's face as she had whispered, *I can still taste you.*

"That's what I'm talking about." Gretchen's voice in her ear snapped her back to the present. "You need to think about coming back to the city. With the article out, there's no reason for you to stay away."

"I'll think about it," Cori promised before hanging up.

Maybe Gretchen was right. The article was out. People had already read it. It was a good article, she admitted. Two days after her departure, Ben had sent the draft in for Cori's approval. Cori had been pleased with Ben's work, finding the article to be accurate, detailed, and still respectful of her privacy. She had asked for only a couple of minor changes, and surprisingly, Ben made them with no argument.

Fingering the business card she still held in her hand, Cori wished she could call Ben and ask her why she hadn't fought the changes. She wished she could call her and…just talk. If only things were that simple. Shaking her head, she consciously changed her line of thinking. Things weren't simple. For a start, she had no right even thinking about inviting someone into her life, such as it was.

She wandered out onto the deck and leaned against the railing, staring off into the distance. Pushing a hand through her hair, she decided she'd been doing entirely too much of this lately. She'd never spent so much time staring into space. Usually a woman of action, she suddenly found herself completely unable to make the simplest of decisions without overanalyzing things.

She thought again about Gretchen's parting request. She could go back. She'd have to face everyone eventually and it was probably time. Maybe returning to her old life would be just what she needed. Yes, going back and resuming her social activities would certainly leave no room for all this introspection she seemed prone to recently.

❖

After quickly draining the glass in her hand, Cori set it on the tray of a passing waiter and grabbed a full one. She smoothed her hand over the front of her silk blouse and turned to survey the room. As the rush of alcohol hit her system, she began to relax. This was where she belonged. The events of the past few months had thrown her off balance, but now she was back in her element.

"Hey, kiddo, you might want to slow down on those," Gretchen said in her ear as she stepped close behind her.

To prove a point, Cori tossed back the rest of her drink and turned to face her friend. Rediscovered confidence rushing through her system, she gave her a slow, sexy smile. Gretchen looked stunning as usual in a simple black cocktail dress that complemented her petite frame, her dark hair swept back from her face.

She, like Cori, had been born and bred for a life of leisure. Their mothers had never been interested in careers, instead spending their days shopping or at the club playing tennis. Gretchen and Cori were raised to follow the same path, but neither had. If asked why, Gretchen would say that she hated tennis. Cori had never been able to be as flippant about her reasons. She knew only that since she was a child, the urge to express herself had been a strong force within her. Both women worked hard, but they played hard as well, thoroughly enjoying the privileges life afforded them.

"I'm serious, Cori. I'm glad you're back, but you need to take it easy." Her tone was light and free of judgment, but Cori detected a note of concern.

"Now, Gretchen, when have you ever known me to take it easy at one of these things?" Cori gestured broadly around the room. The impromptu cocktail parties were common among their circle of friends. Their hostess had opened her opulently decorated home to fifty of her closest friends and their dates. The large open area boasted an ornately carved bar along one side of the room and a huge ebony grand piano tucked in a corner. Textured wallpaper and red velvet drapes made the air in the room feel thick—stuffy. Garish gold candlesticks held heavily scented candles. A collection of nineteenth-century sculptures was a testament to the owner's affluence. Cori's practiced eye picked out a particularly impressive Rodin displayed on a pedestal nearby.

"God, look at this place," she muttered to herself.

"That's my point, sweetie." Gretchen ignored her look of disgust. "Things aren't the same as they used to be. You aren't the same."

"I'm exactly the same," Cori argued, though she knew it was a lie. She wasn't. The *old Cori* walked into a room and commanded it, earning admiring and envious looks. *This Cori* got looks of pity, and that was just from the people who didn't avoid eye contact. That knowledge seared into her, cementing her resolve to prove she was just as strong as she had once been. She caught herself stiffening her spine, and in an attempt to ease the rigidity of her posture, she rolled her shoulders and slipped her hand into the pocket of her slacks.

"I know that look." Gretchen tucked her hand in the crook of Cori's elbow. "Please, take it easy."

"Just last week you were telling me I needed to get back to the city. Now I'm here and you're trying to rein me in. Make up your mind."

Relenting, Gretchen slid her hand up to squeeze Cori's bicep. "Enjoy yourself. You deserve it."

"I think I will." Cori handed her empty glass to Gretchen. "And I'm going to start over there." She nodded toward a corner of the room occupied by several attractive women.

Flashing Gretchen one of her trademark grins, Cori pushed back her shoulders and strode into the crowd. The swagger that had once been second nature now required conscious thought, but she was certain she was pulling it off.

Halfway across the room, Cori lifted another glass from the tray of a passing waiter. Too late she caught sight of Alyson Haines approaching her. Alyson was the wife of Edward Haines, head of Dexcon, a Fortune 500 textiles company. Pasting a polite smile on her face, Cori gulped down a good amount of the champagne.

"Cori, darling. I was saddened to hear of your dreadful affliction," Alyson cooed as she halted just outside of touching range. Her formal speech and exaggeratedly Waspish accent always made Cori wonder if anyone *really* talked like that.

"It's not contagious, Alyson," she said wryly. At any other time Alyson would have swept her up in an embrace. In fact, the lithe brunette had no aversion to close physical contact on several occasions Cori could recall.

"Of course not." Alyson backpedaled. "I'm merely trying to express my concern."

"Sure you were," Cori bit back sarcastically.

"You know, I don't think your illness is an excuse for rudeness." Alyson's defensive tone was no doubt intended to chastise. However, it only made Cori more aware of just how superficial her world really was. She was not in the mood for these social games.

For the next couple of hours, she drifted around the room draining glass after glass of champagne. She flirted endlessly, attempting to convince herself that she didn't feel the helplessness growing inside of her. But she did. She felt it every time someone made even the most casual reference in conversation to Ben's article. She felt it in the pitying gazes of the other guests when they thought she wasn't looking. She thought she had taken back some of the control she'd lost when she was diagnosed. However, as she was finding out, nothing she did could ease the aching knot that grew tighter every day.

She was on the verge of a serious case of self-pity when she felt a hand curl teasingly around her arm. As she turned, her eyes drifted lazily over a compact but curvaceous figure. The woman's body was practically poured into an electric blue sleeveless number. The top was cut low enough to reveal a good amount of cleavage, and the hem rode high on her shapely thighs.

"I'm Veronica," the blonde purred, running a manicured fingernail over Cori's collar.

"Cori."

"Oh, I know who you are." Trailing her fingers over Cori's forearm, she lifted the empty glass from Cori's hand and smoothly replaced it with a full one.

Cori raised blurry eyes to met Veronica's green ones and saw the familiar glint of lust in them. Too much champagne had dulled her senses, but she was still lucid enough to recognize the invitation in Veronica's eyes. *She's not what you're looking for,* her conscience whispered. However, it was quickly stifled by the memory of her recently developed penchant for self-doubt. She had something to prove to herself, and this attractive woman was presenting an opportunity to do just that. Cori didn't stop to feel guilty because she was certain Veronica's expectations didn't extend much past this one night and her interest didn't go deeper than Cori's celebrity status.

❖

Cori barely had time to close the door to Veronica's apartment when the shorter woman was on her, pushing her back against the wall. She leaned into Cori, fastening her mouth on the side of her neck. Cori intercepted the hands that reached for her blouse. She shook her head at Veronica's questioning look and said roughly, "That's not how I want it."

"What do you want, baby?" Veronica allowed Cori to steer her toward the bedroom.

"I want you to do as I say." Cori had spent the entire cab ride home trying to keep Veronica's wandering hands under control. Now she was desperately trying to get her to the bed before she lost the battle and Veronica took her against the wall of her apartment. Veronica was obviously an extremely practiced seductress, but Cori was fast discovering it wasn't Veronica's hands she wanted on her. In fact, she was not enjoying her touch at all, and just wanted this to be over.

Pushing her back until her knees hit the edge of the bed, Cori pulled down the zipper at the back of Veronica's dress. After the garment fell around Veronica's ankles, Cori pushed her back onto the bed. When Veronica reached for her, Cori caught her wrists and pinned them over her head.

"Don't touch me," Cori ordered, pleased to see obedience shining in Veronica's eyes. She had played this game before, and she wouldn't touch until she was allowed. Cori released her wrists, confident that they would remain in place.

Champagne still racing through her blood, she pulled her unfocused gaze from Veronica's face. Normally she would revel in the reactions of her partner. She was aware of each twitch and sigh and very much enjoyed giving that pleasure. Tonight, though, she wouldn't watch Veronica's face as she touched her. She didn't need to see Veronica's eyes change and go hazy with passion; the face that danced at the edges of her consciousness wasn't Veronica's. Cori squeezed her eyes shut and edged out that image before it could fully develop.

Shaking her head, she bent over and abruptly pulled one of Veronica's nipples between her lips, sucking harshly. The other woman gasped at the sudden and unexpected contact, but Cori did not waver. She alternately teased and pulled relentlessly. It wasn't until Veronica's back arched and a litany of incoherent pleading fell from her lips that Cori pushed her palm flat against Veronica's stomach, holding her in place while she slid her mouth lower.

When Cori reached the sensitive flesh along the insides of her thighs, Veronica's hips came off the bed. Still anchored by Cori's spread fingers in the center of her abdomen, she struggled to push herself closer to Cori's teasing lips and tongue, a low moan escaping as teeth scraped against tender skin.

"Oh, not so fast, I'm going to come," Veronica pled.

Cori slowed only for a second, drawing Veronica to the edge, but she would not linger long. Wedging her shoulders between Veronica's thighs, Cori spread them apart. She did not go gently, curling her lips firmly around Veronica's clitoris and sucking. Veronica's hips bucked beneath her, but Cori simply held her pinned there and marveled at the fact that Veronica's hands remained above her head. Cori was certain that if Veronica were not so practiced in submission, her hands would be buried in the back of Cori's hair.

Sensing that the eager blonde was on the edge, Cori quickly shoved three fingers deep inside her and raked her teeth over the pulsing flesh in her mouth. Veronica's thighs surged against Cori's shoulders and her back curved violently as she shuddered and cried out.

As her cries subsided into soft sounds of lingering pleasure, Cori withdrew her fingers, lifted herself on her arms, and crawled up Veronica's supine body. She leaned down and swiped her tongue firmly over the sweat-dampened skin between Veronica's breasts. When Veronica lifted her head for a kiss, Cori moved away. Still fully clothed, she left the room without a backward glance at the woman sprawled on the bed behind her.

Outside Veronica's apartment building, Cori opted to walk the ten blocks to her place, hoping the cool night air would help clear her head. The encounter with Veronica had been similar to dozens of others she'd had. It should have been equally satisfying. *So why do I feel so mixed up? This doesn't make any sense. I'm not symptomatic, and it's not like Veronica would have noticed if I was.* Could that be it? The thought stopped her short in the middle of the street. What difference should it make to her that Veronica wasn't more considerate of her? It didn't make any difference. They both knew what they wanted when they left that party together. And as always, Cori had delivered exactly what her reputation promised. So why wasn't that enough? It always had been before.

By the time she pushed open the door to her own apartment, Cori's buzz had worn off. In the kitchen she found a half-full bottle of tequila and knocked back a healthy shot. She welcomed the fiery path as it burned down her throat.

A couple of drinks later she was sprawled on the living-room floor, her back against the couch. The face that had threatened to intrude earlier now drifted through her mind and she let herself dwell on the myriad of Ben's expressions, from the cool professionalism tinged with skepticism of their first meeting to the heavy-lidded arousal following their kiss on the boat.

She felt guilty about Veronica, which was ridiculous. She and Ben didn't have any claim on each other. So why did she feel unfaithful? *Hell, for all I know, she's out there doing the same thing right now.* What did she *really* know about Bennett McClain? She knew nothing of her personal life or reputation. Ben could be as much of a player as Cori was, she just wasn't as high profile.

Another shot of tequila did little to soothe the jealousy that rose up at the thought of Ben having sex with someone else. *This is crazy,* she thought as she dragged herself to the bedroom. *So what if I think she's attractive? I can even admit I want to sleep with her. That doesn't make her any different than a dozen other women.*

CHAPTER TEN

"Have you seen the tabloids lately?" Lucy asked hesitantly as Ben reached for the carton of fried rice.

They were back to their routine of Wednesday lunches in Lucy's office. Ben had stopped for Chinese takeout on her way over. Several opened cartons littered the glass coffee table in front of them.

Ben glanced around, realizing how much she missed the comfort of this routine whenever it was interrupted. Lucy had moved into the large office a year before when she made partner at the law firm. The décor was similar to Lucy's apartment. She favored a lot of blacks and whites with carefully chosen splashes of color. The walls were painted white and the furniture was black. The only spot of color in the room was a large, deep red vase that stood next to the black lacquer bookcase. A leather sofa and chair and coffee table created an inviting sitting area in one corner. Lucy's glass-topped desk sat in front of the large windows. Ben knew that when she was puzzling over something, Lucy liked to twirl around in her chair, alternately studying the city outside and whatever perplexing case lay on her desk.

"Just the covers as I went past the newsstand," Ben replied dryly.

She knew what Lucy was getting at. Just that morning, she had stopped dead in the middle of the sidewalk as she stared at the cover of *Exposure*. Ignoring the irritated mutters of people forced to change course quickly to get around her, she had been unable to move or think for several seconds. If it weren't for the two other women in the photo flanking Cori, Ben might have said it wasn't a bad picture. But the photographer had either failed to capture the intensity that burned in Cori's eyes, or it had been lacking when this photo was taken.

"Cori Saxton is back in town."

"I know."

"And it looks like she is back to her old self again." Lucy glanced at Ben.

"I know," Ben said tightly.

Setting down the carton, the contents of which she had been poking listlessly with her chopsticks, she sighed and let her shoulders droop. She didn't worry about trying to hide her emotions from Lucy. Her cousin had drilled her endlessly during her first few days back from upstate and Ben had given up most of the details of her time with Cori.

"I guess it was inevitable," Lucy said.

"Do you think it's true?"

Lucy's sympathetic expression was answer enough. Disheartened, Ben slid deeper into the oversized leather couch. Lucy pushed back next to her and covered Ben's hand with hers.

"I just hate to see her selling herself short," Ben remarked, attempting to downplay her disappointment. This should make things easier. Knowing that in all likelihood the vulnerability she thought she had glimpsed that last night had probably been an act should make it easier for her to move on. So why did she still find herself thinking entirely too much about the artist? Why did it seem she was unable to keep her mind from replaying their shared kiss? Why did she continue to think about the fear that shone in Cori's eyes as she had revealed the nature of her illness?

"You care for her?"

"Yes," Ben answered without hesitation. "As irrational as it seems, I do care for her."

"Can you deal with her being ill?" Lucy asked the question that had been lingering in the back of Ben's mind.

"I don't know."

Both women were silent. Ben suspected they were both thinking of the same thing—Randall. Lucy had been there and had seen the devastation Ben had felt as a child going through her brother's illness.

"What are you working on now?"

Ben smiled, aware that Lucy was changing the subject.

"I'm doing a story on Brian Cobb." The politician was a favored candidate for an open senate seat in the upcoming election.

"He's a *Republican*," Lucy spat the word out as if its very pronunciation repulsed her.

"I didn't say I was voting for him, I'm just writing about him," Ben defended. "Besides, I find his ideas on immigration interesting."

"Yeah, well, I find his ideas on gay marriage much more interesting," Lucy argued.

"There is that."

"Yes, there is." Lucy's eyes narrowed and she was obviously awaiting an explanation.

"Ah, the truth is," Ben began hesitantly, "I got offered the article and I needed something to occupy my mind, so I took it. Besides, I'm not writing in support of him. It's merely a very short informative piece."

"Hmph." A grunt was Lucy's only response. But Ben took her lack of further argument as understanding, if not acceptance.

Their conversation about Cori was on Ben's mind for the rest of the day. During her interview with Cobb and his wife, she constantly had to jerk her attention back to the couple in front of her. Just when she was able to get her concentration back on track, something would trigger thoughts of Cori again.

She needed to stop at the market on the way home, and her detour took her past the newsstand down the street again. Cori's face jumped out from the cover of the tabloid. It was clear the photo was taken at a lavish party. Cori's vacant expression was likely due to whatever was in the glass she raised. *DROWNING HER TROUBLES?* Ben cringed at the headline, wondering how much her article had contributed to the renewed interest in Cori's "troubles." She didn't question her motives as she handed a couple of bills to the newsagent.

Ben pushed open the door to her apartment and headed for the kitchen. She deposited the bags of groceries on the counter and dropped the tabloid next to them. While unpacking the groceries, she ignored the picture staring back at her. Still unsure why she'd even bought the rag, she hadn't been able to bring herself to actually read the article.

She spent the next hour roaming around the apartment restlessly pretending to straighten the already spotless living room. The constant travel that her work required left her with little time to spend at home. Perhaps because of that, she appreciated even more the time she did get. By her friends' standards her apartment was small, but Ben had fallen in love with it the moment she had seen it. She'd had no qualms about spending a large chunk of her savings on a down payment. The renovated apartment in a prewar building on the Upper East Side boasted high ceilings, hardwood floors, and an oversized bathtub. The galley-style kitchen was on the small side but, if she was being honest, Ben didn't spend too much time in the kitchen anyway. Over the years, she had lovingly decorated with a collection of mismatched antiques that she'd found on her travels.

Her eyes kept straying back to the newsprint image as she worked. "This is ridiculous," she muttered, finally deciding a bath might take her mind off Cori. It usually helped her to unwind after a long day.

She drew a bath, adding some scented bath salts, and poured herself a glass of wine. Before long, fragrant steam drifted throughout the room. She lit some candles, stripped off her clothes, and slid into the tub. The soothing water immediately began to melt the knots of tension from her muscles. She tilted her head back to rest on the edge and closed her eyes. As her frustration slipped away, Ben sighed and sank deeper until the water touched the tips of her earlobes. The tightness in her neck eased and the edges of her mind blurred, unfocused in her relaxation.

When Cori's face swam unbidden behind her closed eyes, Ben did not force the image away. She did not see the face from the cover of the tabloid. She saw Cori as she was on Janet's boat, pulling herself out of the water after their swim, all bronzed lean limbs, muscles flexed, beads of water dancing across the surface of her skin as she hefted herself up the ladder and into the boat.

Under the pleasant heat of the afternoon sun, Ben had been hypnotized when Cori had stroked her fingers over her shoulder and then into her hair. She hadn't had any defenses against the weight of Cori's body against her, both comforting and arousing. Now, weeks later, she slid upward again on a slowly cresting wave of arousal, as gentle as those rocking the boat. She was just as helpless now to deny her need as she had been then. She relived that urge to close the distance between them without a thought for consequence. She had needed Cori's lips against hers and Cori's skin beneath her fingertips. She still did.

As the memory of Cori's mouth opening for her flooded back, Ben slipped her hand beneath the water. As her mind conjured up the images of what might have happened had Janet not interrupted them, she rubbed her fingers over her nipple. She imagined Cori's hands on her shoulders, pushing her back against the seat of the boat. Ben brushed her hand over her abdomen, envisioning the sleek warmth of Cori's back. And when she pushed her hand between her thighs she imagined that Cori's fingers stroked over her clitoris, somehow knowing just how much pressure would bring Ben right to the edge without putting her over.

She jerked her hand away and sat up straight, startled by the ringing of her cell phone from the next room. Deciding that by the time she got out of the tub and retrieved the phone she would have missed the call anyway, she let it go to voicemail. The interruption had effectively broken the spell cast by the wine and warm water. She stared at her hand accusingly, as if it had acted entirely on its own. However, she couldn't forget the images that had played in her head. *Oh hell, what was I doing? Fantasizing about a woman I can't even stand?*

That was not entirely true, Ben admitted as she stood and reached for a towel. There were many things about the public Cori Saxton that Ben didn't like. But she couldn't ignore the fact that she had seen another side of her, and she didn't think that private self was an act. She had seen a strong woman covering up a core of vulnerability. She had seen a kind, thoughtful woman. She had seen a passionate, intense woman. Cori had dimensions that the press had never seen, or if they had, had chosen not to write about. Ben had glimpsed them and she had been taken in from that moment on.

She pulled on a thick robe and reminded herself that she would never see Cori Saxton again. She carried her half-finished glass of wine out to the kitchen, picking her cell phone up on the way. Mitchell had left a message. He wanted her to accompany him to a party the next weekend, as a thank-you for a job well done with the article. She decided she would call him back later.

A glance at the clock told her the night was still young. *And here I am, ready to turn in for the evening. No wonder I'm obsessing about someone I can't be with. It's Friday night and I have absolutely no plans.* Recently, she'd fallen into a routine and was spending more and more time alone. *Maybe that's what I need, a night out.* Her mind made up, she stripped off her robe and began sorting through her closet.

❖

The music that pounded out into the street when the door to the club was opened was nearly enough to make Ben change her mind. Maybe she should have picked one of the more laid-back bars. *No, I can do this.* The repetitive thump of the bass seemed to vibrate the very air around her. The room was filled with mostly twentysomething women, most of whom were grinding against each other on the dance floor. Ben knew she was going to need more than a glass of wine if she was going to stay here for long. Winding her way through a throng of bodies, she headed straight for the bar.

As she slid into an empty space and waved to the bartender, a woman a few stools down caught her eye. Black over-gelled hair stood up in spikes and dark eyes were ringed by too much eyeliner. But there was something about the indolent way she slouched against the bar that drew Ben's eyes to her body. Her hips were cocked to one side and her thumb hooked on the pocket of frayed blue jeans.

Ben had never seen the woman before, but there was something familiar about her.

The harried bartender leaned in her direction, and on a whim, Ben called out her order as well as instructions to replenish the slouching woman's drink. She watched as the drink was served and the bartender hitched a thumb in her direction. An indifferent gaze lifted to meet hers and Ben forced a smile. The woman lifted her chin ever so slightly. Ben wasn't certain it was an invitation but she took it as one anyway. A diversion. This was what she needed. She moved down the bar.

"Thanks," the woman said as Ben drew close. "What's your name?"

"Ben."

"Really?" There was a flicker of interest in the nearly ebony eyes.

"Yeah."

"I'm Rachel. How come I've never seen you here before?"

"It's my first time." Ben was barely able to contain a grin at the obvious line. The measured smile on Rachel's lips said she thought she was smooth. Ironically, Ben had come to the club to get Cori Saxton off her mind and ended up chatting up a woman who fancied herself a player. Only she wasn't, not really. Whereas Cori's charisma was natural, an innate part of her, Rachel's seemed contrived. She was a young buck playing a part.

"Are you new in town?"

"No. But I travel a lot for work, so I'm not around much."

"Really, what do you do?"

"I'm a journalist."

"That must be an interesting job." Rachel smiled.

"Sometimes. What about you?"

"Oh, nothing exciting. I'm a paralegal." She gestured at Ben's empty glass. "Can I get you a refill?"

"Um, sure." This wasn't going quite how Ben had planned. She had expected a more aggressive come-on—something anonymous. Sure, there was an underlying flirtation to the woman's words and the none-too-subtle way she slid closer when she called out their drink order to the bartender. But she also seemed interested in their conversation.

When their drinks were delivered, Rachel took a sip before turning to Ben with a raised eyebrow. "Would you like to dance?"

Ben smiled. Rachel's cocky expression made it clear that she didn't expect to be refused. She nodded and allowed Rachel to take her hand and lead her to the dance floor. Taking the opportunity, she slid her eyes down Rachel's narrow back. The baggy jeans hanging just under the waistband of a pair of boxers did nothing for her figure. Ben couldn't help but make a comparison to the way Cori wore her jeans, as if they were made for her lean hips. Cori's swagger fit her in a way that Rachel's contrived gait never would. *I cannot be so obsessed with Cori that I can't even get her out of my head long enough to get interested in someone else.* By any standards, Rachel was an attractive woman. It was only when compared to the mysterious artist who oozed sex appeal that she could be found lacking. *So stop comparing them, damn it. And just enjoy the attentions of a sexy younger woman.*

As one song faded into another one, Rachel pulled her close, and Ben automatically matched the movement of her hips to the other woman's. She slid her hands around Rachel's waist and tried to keep her mind on the woman in front of her. Soon she was able to let herself go, feeling only the pulsing music and the slender body pressed against hers.

"You're a good dancer." The whisper of breath as Rachel spoke close to Ben's ear sent a shiver down her spine. It was a purely physical reaction, but it was enough for her.

They danced through three more songs, each pushing the flirtation a little bit further. When Rachel's hands wandered down past her lower back, Ben slid her hand to the back of Rachel's neck, teasing the fine hair in encouragement. Rachel's lips brushed her neck and Ben pressed closer until she knew the other woman could feel her breasts against her chest. Rachel's mouth covered Ben's, her tongue pushing past her lips. Here was the aggression she'd been seeking. The jolt of pleasure, the sudden throbbing between her thighs could prove to be just the distraction she needed. Ben's fingers dug into the back of Rachel's neck as she met the bruising kiss.

Rachel backed off long enough to speak. "Unless you're into public displays, we should take this someplace more private."

"What did you have in mind?" Ben teased. She slid her thigh between Rachel's and was rewarded with a low moan.

"My place is just around the corner."

"Lead the way."

Rachel snaked her arm around Ben's waist and kept it there as she guided her out of the club and down the street. She released Ben long enough to fish a set of keys out of her pocket and let them in.

The door opened into the kitchen and Ben wandered in ahead. The sudden break from Rachel's warm proximity threatened to bring reality rushing back. Immediately Ben moved closer again, trapping Rachel against the counter. She didn't stop to wonder if the groan that issued forth was caused by the thrust of her hips against Rachel's or the pressure from the edge of the counter in the small of the other woman's back. She crushed her mouth against Rachel's, biting at her lower lip.

"If we don't slow down, I'm going to have you right here in my kitchen." Rachel sucked in a ragged breath when Ben's hands pushed beneath her T-shirt. She reversed their position and urged Ben up to sit on the counter.

"And that would be bad because..."

Rachel moved between Ben's thighs and tugged her closer until Ben's crotch was snug against her midsection.

"Not bad—definitely not bad," Rachel managed between nipping at Ben's neck.

Ben's head fell back. But when she closed her eyes, Cori's face swam behind them. Her expression was arrogant, as if she knew Ben was trying, unsuccessfully, to drive her out of her head. *It won't work.* In Ben's mind, Cori glanced dismissively at Rachel. *Is* this *really what you want?* Her expression said she knew it wasn't.

When Ben snapped her eyes open, the accusing stare lingered. "Damn it." She pushed Rachel back and slid off the counter.

"What's wrong?"

"Nothing." She drew Rachel toward her again and fused her mouth to Rachel's neck.

"Mmm, baby," Rachel moaned, but it was Cori's voice that she heard, low and husky.

"Fuck." She jerked out of Rachel's arms.

Rachel stepped back and waited. "What's happening?"

"I'm sorry. I can't do this."

"Did I do something wrong?" The wounded look on the young woman's face made Ben feel guilty.

"Not at all. Jesus, I can't believe I'm saying this but, it's not you, it's me."

"Sure, right." Disbelief shone in Rachel's eyes. Despite her cocky exterior, she'd obviously been hurt before and Ben had just repeated someone else's mistake. Her guilt increased exponentially as she realized that her misguided attempt at beating Cori at her own game had caused pain to this sweet woman.

"I'm really sorry. I thought this was about you and me, but—I just wasn't ready for this. And that's not fair to you. You deserve more than that." Ben laid her palm lightly against Rachel's cheek, trying to take the sting out of the situation.

"Yeah, okay." Rachel moved away. "I think you should go now."

In the end, the solitary cab ride home was sobering. Swamped with regret for what she'd done and what she'd *almost* done, Ben resolved to do whatever it took to get Cori out of her head. She would focus on her career. And she would start by going to that party with Mitchell. Maybe she could cultivate some new contacts and generate some more work in the art scene.

The click of the lock disengaging echoed through Cori's head, yanking her out of a near-sound sleep. Seconds later she heard the door to her apartment open and then close much too loudly. Groaning, she rolled over and pulled a pillow over her head.

"Cori," Gretchen sang out from the other room.

"Ugh, kill me now," Cori muttered through layers of cotton and feathers.

"Oh, here you are." Gretchen sank down on the bed beside her. "You missed breakfast with Barbara," she scolded. "She was asking about you."

"Tell her I died."

"You don't think this grumpy bit is cute, do you?"

"Remind me again, why did I give you a key to my place?"

"Because you don't want your plants to die," Gretchen supplied helpfully.

Spending so much time away from the apartment that she kept in the city necessitated handing over a key to someone. And in an apparent moment of insanity Cori had thought Gretchen a good candidate.

Gretchen unrolled the top of the paper bag she was holding.

"Please, stop," Cori begged, flailing blindly with her hand in an effort to stop the offending noise.

"Come out from under there. I brought muffins and coffee, though it's really past lunchtime now."

"Coffee?" Cori stuck her head out from under the pillow, sniffing the air appreciatively.

"How are we feeling today?" Gretchen asked in mock sympathy, holding a Styrofoam cup just out of Cori's reach.

"Don't be a tease." Cori lunged for the cup in vain. Gretchen grinned and held it away from her. Cori pulled herself gingerly into a sitting position.

"Oh, all right." Gretchen handed over the cup and waited while Cori pried off the lid and inhaled deeply.

"Perfect." The aroma of rich coffee and hazelnut seduced her, almost managing to take her mind off the pounding in her head. She took a sip and sighed as the warm liquid eased her dry mouth and throat. "Did you say you had muffins?"

Gretchen handed over the bag and slid to the empty side of the bed to settle next to her. "Where did you run off to last night?"

Cori looked up from the blueberry muffin she was pulling apart. "I, uh, had to escort Veronica home." She shoved a piece of muffin into her mouth.

"Hmm. Okay. Give," Gretchen demanded.

"Oh, hell." Cori pushed a hand through her hair. When Gretchen remained silent, she went on. "I thought…" Her voice trailed off.

"What were you trying to accomplish?"

"I was just trying to make things normal again." Cori set her coffee cup on the nightstand.

"Oh, sweetie." Gretchen didn't offer platitudes or false assurances. She opened her arms and waited while Cori settled against her. "Did it work?"

"No," Cori admitted, her face pressed into Gretchen's neck.

CHAPTER ELEVEN

Cori steered her black Jaguar XK convertible into the U-shaped drive in front of Gretchen's house. Choosing to park the car near the garage rather than trust it to the valets Gretchen had hired for the party, she eased into the space next to Gretchen's Mercedes. She got out and glanced back as she engaged the alarm.

The car had been a gift to herself last year in celebration of her first show to gross six figures. She had enjoyed leafing through the brochures for hours, picking out just the right features, finally deciding on the sleek ebony exterior, charcoal leather interior with aluminum trim, 20" Senta wheels, and a 525-watt, eight-speaker Alpine sound system. She'd had a state-of-the-art navigation system installed aftermarket and took perhaps too much pleasure in the woman with the English accent telling her when to turn right. Grinning to herself as she thought of the sexily accented voice, Cori strode toward the house.

After the fiasco with Veronica, she had been hesitant to attend another party. It would be the same social circle that she was tired of. She'd given up on thinking she could make herself feel normal by going through the same old routines.

But Gretchen was hosting the party and had been planning it for weeks. Cori was well aware that everyone would expect her to be there, and they would all have plenty of questions for her. Not about her work, however. That topic suddenly seemed to be out of bounds. Gretchen had reeled off the names of some powerful people in the art world who were on the guest list. Normally Cori would have been excited about being in their company, but what was she going to say? She couldn't talk about her next show, or a new technique she was experimenting with.

She was here only because she didn't want to let Gretchen down. But tonight she didn't want to be Cori Saxton. She would play the role for as long as she could, but her plan was to slip away as soon as possible.

❖

Ben wandered away from Mitchell, lifting her glass at his questioning look to indicate she needed a refill. As she moved among the crowd, she smoothed her hand self-consciously across the back of her neck and down her side. She had swept her hair up and pinned it up in a simple yet elegant style. Though she knew that the rich chocolate color of her dress complimented her complexion and its simple lines flattered her figure, she still felt completely out of place. She recognized the work of several top-name designers hugging bodies no doubt surgically sculpted. The teardrop-shaped diamond that hung on a silver chain around her neck felt plain in a room full of expensively jeweled guests.

She stood at the bar along the far wall, awaiting her drink, when a shiver of awareness danced along her spine. Turning, she scanned the crowd and focused on the front door just as Cori walked through it. Confident that Cori was unaware of her gaze, Ben allowed her eyes to roam hungrily over her. Cori wore a black tuxedo-cut pantsuit, perfectly pressed with sharp creases. Her white shirt was a stark contrast to her tanned skin and her blond hair was slightly shaggy, obviously not having been cut since Ben had last seen her. The sexily mussed style still appeared to be deliberate and definitely didn't detract from her allure.

Standing unobserved across the room, Ben was still deciding whether she should approach or avoid Cori when a dark-haired woman stepped up next to Cori. The woman looked incredible in a knee-length red dress. The halter style top showed off strong shoulders, and the flared skirt swirled around her legs. She touched

Cori's arm and there was affection in her eyes as she tilted her head back to look at her.

The easy intimacy between the two women had Ben's insides twisting in jealousy. When Cori walked away, her companion looked up and caught Ben staring. She looked away quickly.

Smiling, the woman closed the distance between them.

"I don't think we've been properly introduced. I'm Gretchen Mills." A slim, fine-boned hand slid gracefully into Ben's.

Though she suspected that Gretchen knew exactly who she was, Ben said, "Bennett McClain."

She recognized the woman as Cori's agent and their hostess for the evening. She smiled politely in response to Gretchen's obvious social ease. Remembering the familiar way she touched Cori's arm, Ben thought that Gretchen was probably the type of woman Cori would go for—socially adept and polished. She refused to examine her disappointment as she realized she was neither of those things and probably never would be.

Her eyes darted back to Gretchen's face when she heard the other woman chuckle softly. Gretchen cocked her head to the side in a gesture that reminded Ben of Cori. "You're trying to decide if Cori and I have ever been romantically involved." It was not a question but a statement, and was said without rancor and with a touch of amusement. Ben did not respond. "We haven't."

"It's none of my business," Ben said despite the relief that washed over her.

"Yeah, sure," Gretchen murmured without an ounce of sincerity before excusing herself and moving away to greet another guest.

Ben's eyes drifted back across the room. She allowed herself to admire for a moment the way Cori moved about the room, flowing sinuously between small groups of people. She seemed inordinately aware of her body and moved as if every motion was deliberate and effortless. This was the Cori Saxton she'd expected to find when she stepped out of Henry Rollins's truck weeks ago. Confident, her presence seeming to fill the room. Here was the artist envied by her peers and lusted after by men and women alike. Seeing Cori in her element, larger than life, Ben could see why. Her smooth, subtly sexy walk brought to mind images of that body sliding against Ben's own. The room seemed to grow warmer as her pulse accelerated.

Ben watched heads turn as Cori passed and was certain she was not the only person suddenly finding all of her blood rushing south to pulse between her thighs. But she was probably the only one to recognize the vulnerability Cori worked so hard to hide. She had witnessed the fine tremors in Cori's hand and the dark circles of exhaustion and pain beneath her eyes. She had seen agonizing fear swim in her eyes when Cori first talked about her illness. And not one of those things made Ben want her less. They merely added a protective instinct beneath the desire churning within her.

❖

Justin Whitfield had purchased a number of Cori's paintings. They hung in both of his homes as well as several of his offices around the country. This was a compliment. He was a collector whose opinion mattered. Other collectors took notice when he picked up an artist and even now, standing at his side, Cori could feel speculative eyes on her. She felt like making an announcement: *Yes, my paintings will increase in value because that's what happens when there aren't any more.*

Normally an artist had to die to see their works suddenly double in value. Lucky her; she didn't have to wait that long. Justin had just picked one up at auction and was acting like he'd made a killing because anytime soon the Getty people would come knocking at his door. When he was done congratulating himself over that, he moved on to foreign affairs, a topic he said was close to his heart because his father had been a diplomat. Now she was stuck smiling and nodding politely as he spouted his inane ideas about the state of affairs in North Korea.

"Your reporter is here," Gretchen hissed in her ear, barely pausing as she passed by.

Cori jerked her head up, which Justin took to be an awestruck response to his vision of twenty-first-century diplomacy.

"So, as you can imagine I accepted Kim Jong-il's invitation

with an open mind," he waxed on. "His mistress defected to South Korea, you know."

"I didn't realize." Cori scanned the crowd discreetly.

"The Koreans are a fine people," Justin said. "Proud. Disciplined. I brought back some extraordinary ceramic pieces for my Goryeo dynasty collection."

Cori's breath caught in her chest. *She's gorgeous.*

Ben wore a rich brown sheath that hugged her body, cinching slightly at the waist before following her hips and dropping midway down her calves. Her hair was pinned back in a simple style that accentuated the graceful line of her neck. Cori wished she could touch her fingers to that area of skin where the tendrils of hair met the back of Ben's neck.

Cori recognized Mitchell, clad in an expensively cut dark suit, at Ben's side. He glanced at her every few minutes, as if gauging her attention to whatever he was going on about. Several other people gathered around, possibly entranced by his story or by the woman standing next to him. Ben exuded an earthy beauty that contrasted sharply with the superficial glitz around her. She looked warm and real and so desirable, Cori sighed aloud and wondered why she had spent that last night on her boat. It would not have been that hard to seduce her; why had she let the opportunity slip by?

When she intercepted an appreciative stare from an artist she knew vaguely, she excused herself with a quick half-truth about needing some air.

Justin was immediately apologetic. "Is there anything I can do?"

Cori gave him a wistful smile and placed her hand on his arm. "Your support means so much to me. I'll speak to Gretchen. Anything I complete this year…you'll see it first."

Pigs would fly, but her promise had the desired effect. He kissed her hand as if this were a ballroom in Europe and cast a gloating look around the guests milling nearby. A little too loudly, he said, "Consider it sold. I don't have to see a Cori Saxton to know I want it."

Cori scored an approving nod from Gretchen and made her

escape. Ben was still at the center of Mitchell Gardner's clique, and judging by Mitchell's sweeping gestures, he thought he was the life of the party. Ben was doing a good job of concealing her boredom, but Cori could sense a restlessness about her, from the fingers tapping almost imperceptibly against her thigh to the small darting glances around the room. *Is she looking for me?*

When Ben left Mitchell's side, apparently headed for the bar, Cori seized her opening and moved quickly around the perimeter of the room, avoiding eye contact with anyone who made a move toward her. She reached the bar just after Ben and waited among the guests behind her. A tall man greeted a long-lost friend, and Ben hastily took a step back to avoid their reunion. Strong, warm hands gripped her shoulders and her body collided fully with another. "Oh! I'm sorry," Ben began automatically.

"My pleasure," a familiar voice purred in her ear.

Startled, Ben jerked sideways, bumping into a woman with a cocktail in each hand. An embarrassed flush crept up Ben's neck as she mumbled an apology to her as well. She hadn't yet found the strength to raise her eyes.

Cori's heart quickened, keeping pace with her libido. The fleeting sensation of Ben's back pressed to her breasts had ignited every sense in her body. She felt alive, hot, and thrilled.

Flustered, Ben took a few paces toward the wall to escape the jostling. "I didn't know you were here."

"Perhaps that's a good thing," Cori teased gently. "You might not have bothered to come."

If she'd had any doubt about whether Ben wore a bra underneath that dress, she didn't have any now. Ben's nipples altered the silky drape of her cocktail gown and she seemed to be aware of them herself.

Stealing a glance down, Ben said stiffly, "We should move away from these French doors. You must be cold."

"Actually, I'm feeling pretty warm." Cori let her eyes rest on the prominent bumps. She was unable to contain the low moan that vibrated from her throat.

Ben reacted with a sharp intake of breath. "How are you?"

"That question is never just small talk anymore," Cori noted dryly.

Ben lifted her eyes. "No, I guess not." Her gaze raced over that face that had haunted her for weeks. *She looks tired.* Dark circles drew the brilliance from her normally luminous eyes. If possible, she looked even thinner than the last time Ben had seen her, the suit hanging loosely on her shoulders. Ben stepped closer. "Are you ill?"

She had to know. Unable to keep from touching her, Ben brushed her fingers down the outside of Cori's arm, circling her wrist discreetly.

"I'm in remission at the moment." Ironically, she was healthier than she had been since her diagnosis. She was virtually symptom free, and her body had finally seemed to adjust to her medication.

"But you're not sleeping," Ben guessed aloud. It wasn't a question. Cori's drawn look and the hint of fatigue in her posture had given her away.

Cori shrugged. "Not much."

It was a cruel twist that although she was fairly healthy, she had rarely had a full night's sleep since she last saw Ben. She was constantly awakened by dreams that a psychologist would no doubt have a field day with, dreams whose underlying meaning reflected her feelings of inadequacy and fear.

She watched as concern intruded on Ben's cool façade, and for one brief moment she longed to melt into her—to hand herself over to the caring arms of this woman. The warmth of Ben's fingers seeped into her skin and began to unfurl the icy fist that had gripped her insides for months. Cori wanted so much to give in to it, but she could not block out the polite pity she kept seeing on the faces around her. The last thing she wanted was for Ben to look past her as a woman and see only her illness.

She forced herself to meet Ben's eyes, fearing she would find pity there, but Ben was regarding her with a mix of tenderness and dismay that came close to her own. Unusually for her, Cori gave voice to her first thought. "I've missed you."

Ben's throat closed over a rush of emotion and for a moment

she felt like she was drowning. Her voice sounded scratchy as she started to speak. "Cori, I—"

"Cori, darling," a shrill voice cut across Ben as if she were invisible. "I thought you would at least call me after last weekend."

The woman approaching them was walking quickly, considering her three-inch heels and the tight skirt restraining her thighs. Her obviously dyed blond hair was pinned up, leaving several loose tendrils to brush against her exposed neck. Glancing down, Ben realized her neck wasn't the only thing exposed. The top three buttons of her dark green blouse were open, revealing a generous amount of cleavage. She stepped entirely too close to Cori for Ben's liking and draped her arms around Cori's neck as if they always greeted each other like lovers the morning after. Cori turned her head away, and a kiss intended for her mouth landed on her cheek instead.

"How are you, Veronica?" With a quick, embarrassed look at Ben, Cori detached the clinging arms and firmly put some distance between them.

It was naïve to hope that Ben might have missed the innuendo and the possessive way Veronica had just laid claim. Her cold stare made her feelings so plain, Cori was momentarily tongue-tied.

"Oh, I'm sorry. Am I interrupting something?" Veronica acted as if she had just noticed Ben standing there. She gave her a cursory look, clearly dismissing her, and went on before either of them could speak, "I saw you from across the room, Cori darling, and I just had to come over." Undeterred by the previous rebuff, she moved to Cori's side and linked arms with her.

Ben's stomach churned. She desperately needed to escape the situation before she embarrassed herself. *Possibly by throttling the woman right here.* She allowed herself the pleasure of a vivid fantasy, imagining her hands around the busty blonde's throat. But as the woman's face began to turn a lovely shade of blue, she terminated the train of thought. If "Veronica" was Cori's idea of a desirable woman, they deserved each other.

"Well, I will leave you to your…whatever." Lacking the energy to bother with a precise definition, Ben turned to go.

"Ben, wait." Cori extricated herself from Veronica's grasp and took Ben's arm.

"I must be going, anyway." Veronica brushed her lips past Cori's cheek. "Do call me. We have unfinished business."

Ben's icy expression flashed hot as she watched Veronica walk away.

"It's not what you think." Cori stepped closer.

"Well, that *is* a relief. Because I was thinking that you fucked that woman."

"Christ, Ben." Surprised by Ben's bluntness, Cori lowered her eyes. She couldn't lie to her, but still she couldn't quite bring herself to verbally confirm Veronica's insinuations either.

"So, it is, in fact, *exactly* what I think."

Ben didn't need to hear the words; the guilt she'd seen in Cori's eyes before she looked away was sufficient. Her insides shook, but somehow she managed to keep from embarrassing herself with tears. She wasn't certain if she was angrier with Cori or herself. The thought of any woman touching Cori sent a rush of anger and jealousy through her, but realizing that Veronica had been touching Cori just days ago made her absolutely livid. Trying desperately to hold back the flooding rage, Ben once again turned to walk away, and was once again stopped when Cori's hand shot out to roughly grab her wrist.

"Wait, damn it!" Realizing her raised voice had drawn the attention of several people nearby, Cori quickly lowered it again, groping desperately for the words to explain that night. "It was just…sex."

Ben had thought she couldn't be hurt. Anger she could handle, she was familiar with it. But Cori's flippant justification cut deeply. The fact that sex meant so little to her told Ben everything she needed to know about the difference between them. Seething with barely controlled fury, she wrenched her hand away and stepped back. "*Just sex*? Oh, well, that makes it better, doesn't it?"

"I made a mistake." Cori had regretted the encounter with Veronica almost immediately, but this was not the time or place to try to explain that. She needed to talk to Ben in private.

"No, I believe I am the one who made the mistake," Ben shot

back bitterly. "I made the mistake of believing you were different than the shallow, superficial ass I saw in all of those tabloids. But I was wrong. That is exactly who you are."

Cori flinched as if she had been physically struck. Not waiting for a response, Ben turned and stalked away. She almost made it to the door when Mitchell caught her arm, thwarting her dramatic exit. Irritated, she searched his face for any indication that he had seen her exchange with Cori. Excitement gleamed in his features, but she suspected there was another reason for it.

"Where are you going?" he asked, steering her back toward the room.

Sighing, she allowed herself to be led. "I was just going to get some air."

"Well, stick close to me because we're going to line up your next assignment tonight."

"No, I don't think—"

"You're not going to be able to turn this down, Ben, trust me." He negotiated a path to the bar. "I don't know about you, but I need a drink."

Ben accepted the Scotch pressed into her hand a few minutes later and downed it in two swallows. She smacked the glass down soundly on the bar and met the bartender's eyes. "Another. Make it a double."

Mitchell finally seemed to detect that something was wrong. "Listen, if you're worried about that cretin Evander Wynton, don't be. He's the worst kind of poseur. Who cares if he wants to publish a reply to your piece on suburban meth labs. No one's going to read it."

Ben stared at him blankly. "Mitch, I have no idea what you're talking about."

❖

A full, clear moon lit the patio and Cori retreated to a corner shadowed by an ivy-covered trellis. Leaning against the stone wall, she took several deep gulps of the cool evening air.

Ben's parting words echoed in her mind. She knew it made

no sense for her to be upset. She had intentionally set out to prove she was the same as she had ever been, and her illness made no difference. Shouldn't she be thrilled that she had pulled it off? Why should she be huddled out here in a corner, unable to move past the pain she had seen in Ben's eyes?

Why should it sting that Ben walked away from her looking so disillusioned? Who was Ben to her, anyway? Nobody. A journalist who'd written a story about her, that's all. They'd both gone back to their lives. What made Ben think she could judge her for picking up where she left off?

Lost in thought, she only noticed Gretchen standing in front of her when she heard a loud sigh.

"What are you doing, hiding out here? I've been looking all over for you."

"I needed a break. I think I'll go home soon."

"No, you won't...not yet, anyway. Mitchell Gardner wants to meet with us."

"Set something up for next week," Cori said impatiently. She was not in the mood to be nice to anyone else tonight.

Gretchen grasped her hand. "He says it's important, and since he's here and we're here, it may as well be tonight. I told him to meet us in the library in a half hour."

"Gretchen, I know we need to do business, but right now I am just not—"

"This is your career, and let's face it, we're in damage control mode. Mitchell's magazine could do a lot for us."

"In case you haven't noticed, we're doing fine." Cori frowned. "Damage control...what do you mean?"

Gretchen drew her out of the shadows. Her expression was serious. "You're not painting. You know it and I know it, but the rest of the world is expecting another show to be announced sometime soon."

"Well, they can wait. Justin Whitfield says prices are going to go through the roof."

"Which means that people will hold your works. They'll vanish into private collections and you'll become an entry in auction catalogs once or twice a year. Is that what you want?"

Cori knew what Gretchen hadn't said, that for all intents and purposes she was going to be treated like a dead artist in her own lifetime. "No, I don't want that," she said. "But I *can't* paint, so I'm not sure if there's even a choice."

"That's what damage control is about," Gretchen said. "We have to buy time. You *are* going to paint again."

"How can you be so sure?" *I'm not.*

Gretchen gave her a gentle shake. "Because you're an artist and that's what artists do. It's your nature. You might be able to fight it for a while, but you'll never win. None of us do when we're fighting our true natures."

Cori smiled at her friend's sudden fierceness. "I'm not sure if I really know my true nature, but I guess we'll find out. What do you want me to do?"

CHAPTER TWELVE

"Sit down, Mitch, you're making me dizzy." Ben could hear herself slurring, but she seemed to have no control over her tongue. The four glasses of Scotch she had consumed in the past twenty minutes had also loosened her thoughts far too much. And that was nothing compared to the state of her legs.

Unable to stay on her feet for another minute, she dropped down onto the nearest sofa, attempting to appear casual rather than inebriated. This meeting in the library seemed like a crazy idea, and now that the other participants had joined them, the situation had gone from bad to worse. Cori was standing by the windows, as if she wanted to be as far away as possible. Ben could feel her eyes, but she avoided them. This would be over soon. Maybe she could even sleep through it.

"I am sure we can all agree the last article did well. I really think we managed both to expand my readership and ignite Cori's fan base." Mitchell paced the room, obviously pleased with himself and happy to take all the credit. "So, to make a long story short, I think we should do a series of follow-up articles, a sort of a 'week in the life.' Ben would accompany Cori and write several features chronicling events. Readers will eat it up."

"You can't be serious," Ben mumbled. She wasn't sure if anyone heard her.

Mitchell crossed to the chair opposite her and sat down. He gave Ben what he must have thought was a stern look and said,

"There's a lot of buzz. People want to know how Cori is going to manage her illness as she works. This can only be a win/win for all of us."

Ben waved him off. "You mean for your magazine."

Cori barely suppressed a smile. Ben was cute when she was drunk. She was somewhat ambivalent about the "week in the life" idea, but Gretchen looked thrilled. If she tried, she could look like she was working, Cori supposed; she had a few half-finished canvases she could erect around her studio. In still photographs, no one could tell if the paint was fresh. But everything was premised on Ben agreeing to spend the time with her, and Cori couldn't see that happening.

"I want approval," Ben blurted out.

Cori wasn't the only one startled by this demand.

"So you'll do it?" Mitchell sounded astonished.

"I said," Ben repeated very slowly, as if speaking to the developmentally challenged, "I want approval. Period."

Gretchen said, "I don't think that's negotiable. Mitchell, if we agree—"

Panic stole over Mitchell's face. "Ben, be reasonable. Cori only requested the most minor changes to the last piece. You can live with this."

"You're not listening." Ben slid a little farther down the sofa. "What I say goes this time. I get approval or I don't pick up my pen."

She hid a grin with her hand. Cori was never going to buy it. She had lost control over too much to relinquish it for the small stuff. Ben could look good by agreeing to do what Mitchell wanted, and it would be Cori who sabotaged the deal. That was fine with Ben. She had no plans to write a series of articles pretending Cori was a working artist just to make her look good. After tonight, she never wanted to see Cori again.

"Give it to her," Cori said calmly. Ben's eyes flew to hers and held. Cori knew Ben wouldn't be able to read her expression from across the room, but she could feel the questions in that honeyed gaze.

Ben looked dazed. "What?"

"Excellent." Mitchell beamed. "We'll need to start soon or we won't have anything ready for the next issue, of course."

Gretchen was obviously uneasy. "Cori, what we were talking about earlier...I don't want you feeling pressured. This can wait."

Cori understood the last-minute reservations. Gretchen didn't want her to be exposed as not working at all, and if they didn't retain approval they had no control over that. Cori wasn't altogether sure why she was taking such a risk, but she knew one thing: she could not turn down an opportunity to spend more time with Ben. Although Ben's recent words still stung, Cori was sure Ben saw her as more than a selfish socialite, no matter what she wanted to pretend. There was another reason for her outburst, and Cori wanted to hear what it was. She wanted that private conversation.

In a low voice intended only for her, Gretchen asked, "What are you doing?"

"What do you mean? I'm doing exactly what you want me to do. Damage control."

"Explain something to me." Gretchen glanced across the room at Ben, who was in danger of falling off the sofa if she sprawled out any further. "You're over here, sulking and making irrational decisions. She's over there wasted and acting like you're not in the room. Is there something I should know?"

"Mind your own business," Cori snapped.

"You *are* my business." When Cori remained silent, she continued, "Do you think this article is a good idea?"

"Hell, I don't know." It was probably insane to think Ben would change her mind. Maybe she would write a character assassination.

"I can get you out of it," Gretchen said. "It's not like we've signed anything. There's no need for you to make this compromise."

"I think there is."

"I hope you know what you're doing."

"Me too. It's okay, Gretchen." Cori kept her eyes on Ben's face, trying to read beneath her distant expression. "Just make the deal. I'll take care of the rest." With that, she left the library.

Ben stared after her in foggy dismay, barely able to absorb what had just occurred. *I'm going to spend a whole week with Cori Saxton. This can't be happening.*

❖

Another article, what the hell was she thinking? She wanted Ben—that she knew. But the problem was, she wanted her for more than one night, and that was…a relationship. Cori didn't do those, and even if she did, it would be selfish and irresponsible for her to begin one now. She would not subject anyone to a lifetime with an invalid. So why had she just agreed to spend more time with Ben?

Cori watched Ben consume another drink. Ever since she and the others had returned to the party, she'd been a fixture at the bar. Cori had no idea what kind of tolerance Ben had, but she had long ago exceeded it. She scanned the room for Mitchell, wondering when he planned to take Ben home. He was still deep in conversation and didn't appear concerned about Ben's state.

Ben was about to order another drink when she felt someone move behind her. The bartender's gaze slid over her shoulder as if his attention were elsewhere.

"Hey," Ben complained, but he ignored her and set about straightening the bottles. "What the hell—hey, I said I want another drink."

"I think you've had enough." Ben jumped at the words spoken softly in her ear. She spun around and to her dismay stumbled forward directly into Cori's arms. "Damn it," she muttered and struggled to pull back, but Cori didn't let go.

"Whoa. Hold on, let me help you."

"I don't need help." Ben felt a surge of anger, both at Cori for presuming to know how much she should drink and herself for getting into this condition. A bolt of heat shot through her stomach as Cori's warm breath brushed against her ear.

"Do you have a coat?" Cori asked.

"What?"

"When you came in, did you check a coat?"

"No."

Cori glanced in Mitchell's direction once again. He was still oblivious. She tucked Ben against her side and began to steer her toward the door.

"What are you doing?" Ben struggled a bit, but Cori was stronger and kept them on course.

"Taking you home."

"I can get myself home."

"How? It doesn't look like Mitchell is going to be ready to go anytime soon." Cori nodded to Gretchen as they drew close to her. "Tell Mitchell I took her home."

"I'll call a cab," Ben offered uncertainly.

"Why bother? My car is right here." Cori kept a firm grip on Ben's hand and led her down the walk, directing her carefully around the uneven spots. She released Ben long enough to open the car door.

Too drunk to argue, Ben allowed Cori to guide her into the car and close the door. "Don't you have to take Veronica home?" she asked snidely as Cori slid behind the wheel.

"I told you, that didn't mean anything," Cori said wearily.

"And all those women on the magazine covers?"

"Come on, Ben. I'm at a party, some reporter has a camera, and as soon as they start taking pictures everyone is trying to get in them."

"And you're completely innocent, right?" Ben mumbled sarcastically.

Cori didn't respond. She sped out of Gretchen's drive, taking comfort in the aggressive growl of the engine.

"Nice car," Ben slurred after a few beats. "It suits you."

"How's that?"

"Pretentious and flashy." Ben wished she hadn't said that, but she seemed to have lost control of her tongue. She couldn't stop from baiting her.

Cori wasn't biting. She'd been beating herself up over Veronica for the past few days, but she would only make things worse if she tried to explain herself now. Ben was too drunk to listen with her brain turned on, and besides, they would have plenty of time to talk while working together.

They remained silent for the rest of the ten-minute drive, except for Ben muttering the occasional direction. Her apartment was on the Upper East Side, five blocks from Central Park. Cori pulled up to the curb in front of Ben's building. The renovated prewar building boasted a brick and stone façade, partially obscured by the ivy climbing the corner and spreading across the front.

Ben had the door open and was still struggling to climb out of the low car when Cori came around and held out her hand. Though she briefly considered ignoring her, Ben wasn't having much luck extricating herself from the vehicle. She grasped Cori's hand for as long as it took to get out of the car and get her balance, then released it quickly.

"You don't have to walk me up," she said when Cori followed her to the front door.

Her feet betrayed her just as she got the words out and she stumbled on the front steps. Her hand shot out to break her fall, and an arm snaked around her waist, hauling her back. The warm press of Cori's thighs against the back of hers inspired a rush of moisture between her legs. Ben tried to move away, but Cori held her fast.

In her ear, she said, "Let me help you."

Cori hadn't meant to pull Ben quite so tightly against her, but she wasn't quite ready to let her go, either. She'd been caught off guard by the jolt of arousal she felt when Ben's ass came into solid contact with her crotch. Now, holding her close, she felt the curves of Ben's body molding to hers. Her arm was around Ben's waist, just inches from her breasts, supporting her weight. She would only need to slide her hand up slightly to cup one of those breasts. Ben pushed back against her, and Cori cleared her throat in a failed attempt to cover a low groan.

The hum of that groan whispered past Ben's ear and her stomach tightened. Suddenly the buzzing in her head couldn't be blamed completely on the alcohol. She jerked out of Cori's grasp, almost toppling forward before she regained her balance. Grabbing the railing, she fumbled her way up the stairs and unlocked the door without dropping her keys. She hovered in the doorway and turned toward Cori, aware that she should thank her and that she had been unpleasant for the entire ride home. After an awkward silence, they both started to speak at the same time, then fell silent again.

Cori gestured for Ben to go ahead. "You first."

"Okay. I will call you about the article. It's not too late to change your mind, you know." Ben decided she must be sobering up since she had almost managed to inject a professional tone into her voice. She certainly felt anything but professional. Her heart still hammered in her chest and her legs barely supported her. She lacked the concentration to think about something as inane as work when she looked at Cori. There was a flicker of promise in Cori's eyes, a promise that nothing else would matter if only they touched each other again.

"That's fine. Just call my cell and we'll work out a schedule."

Still standing at the bottom of the steps, Cori tilted her head to meet Ben's eyes. Ben's face was flushed and her eyes glassy and Cori hoped it was due, at least in part, to their proximity a moment ago. She could insist on walking Ben up. Ben would invite her in. And then... *Christ, Saxton, she's drunk. That's low, even for you.* Ben had made it quite clear earlier in the evening that she wanted nothing to do with her. *I believe her exact words were "shallow, superficial ass."*

❖

"I don't understand what the problem is."

"You don't understand what the problem is?" Cori followed Gretchen through the seemingly endless booths at the Union Square Farmer's Market a few days after the party.

"Well, you like her, don't you?"

"Do I like her?"

"Okay, you do realize you're just repeating what I'm saying," Gretchen quipped.

"Shut up." Cori paused at a table loaded with various cheeses and picked up a wedge of parmesan. She debated for a moment and then set it down when she found herself wondering if Ben liked fettuccini Alfredo. "Tell me again what we're doing here."

"I told Marianne I could cook, and now she expects me to make dinner for her tonight."

"Wonderful," Cori said. Gretchen had met this woman at the party the previous weekend. She'd been instantly attracted to her and had called Cori the next day to gloat about having a date with the gorgeous redhead. Cori couldn't remember Marianne at all, which astonished her because she would normally have got the number of any sexy woman she ran into, even one Gretchen might be planning to date.

Gretchen wandered to a bin piled high with vine-ripened tomatoes. "I forget, do you squeeze tomatoes and smell melons or is it the other way around?"

"I don't think you're supposed to squeeze or smell tomatoes. Just look for the red ones." Cori picked up two large, red tomatoes and handed them to her. "There's one flaw in your plan. You can't cook."

"I know that and you know that, but she doesn't." Gretchen handed over several bills and took the bag from the vendor. "I talked Louisa into making dinner, but I have to get the ingredients." She consulted the crumpled list in her hand.

"Your housekeeper is cooking dinner for Marianne?"

"Yeah, so?" Gretchen glanced at her before heading off in another direction. "Where do you think they keep the herbs?"

"Well, it's good to know you're basing your relationship on honesty."

Gretchen stopped in the middle of the aisle and Cori stumbled into her. "I'm sorry, are *you* lecturing *me* on honesty?"

"I don't know what you mean. I am absolutely above reproach," Cori shot back.

"Besides, who said I was having a relationship with her?"

"You're a dog."

"My point was, you'll let Ben follow you around for a week. And then it will be over and you can get back to your life." Gretchen paused in front of a table full of fresh herbs.

"I don't know if I even know what that is anymore."

"Sure you do. You've just been distracted." Gretchen bought some herbs and they walked out to her Mercedes.

"I sure have," Cori mumbled.

"So you just spend some time in the city. Stop running off to be a hermit upstate. You'll be back to your old self in no time." Gretchen keyed the remote and popped the trunk.

Cori stood next to the car wondering if her old self was something she wanted to be, even if she had a choice about that. She handed over the packages she'd been carrying and waited while Gretchen stowed them.

"I'm telling you, Cori." Gretchen slammed the trunk and they climbed in. "Just get these new articles over with and we'll deal with the rest. Have you called her yet?"

"Yeah, she's coming over later today so we can make plans." When they'd talked on the phone earlier, Ben had apologized for the way she'd acted during the drive home. They had agreed to make the best of the situation, and Cori was hoping they could have a fresh start.

Gretchen wheeled aggressively into the flow of traffic and Cori cringed as she changed lanes quickly, cutting across within inches of the front bumper of another car.

"God, you're a worse driver than I am," she groaned.

"That's not possible." Gretchen waved away her concern and sped through a yellow light.

❖

Ben stood outside a prewar building on Park Avenue that looked somewhat like her own from the outside, but she knew the inside would be drastically different. Studying its architecture seemed a good stall to keep from going inside. She was second-guessing the drunken bravado that had made her think she could handle this assignment, revisiting her distorted thinking that evening in the library. She had gambled on Cori's refusal and her bluff had blown up in her face. Yet on some level, the gamble was more complicated; she could see that now. She had offered Cori a chance, as if daring her to prove something. She was still shocked that Cori had chosen to take it, to trust her.

Wondering what it meant and why Cori had made that choice,

she took a fortifying breath and entered the building. She gave her name to the doorman. He directed her to the elevator and told her that Ms. Saxton was expecting her. As Ben waited for the doors to close, then listened to the muted whir of the elevator, she felt a heady thrill of anticipation, and it had nothing to do with writing an article. The thought of seeing Cori made her breathless, and when the doors opened on the top floor, she stepped out with a strange sense that nothing in her life was going to be the same again.

Cori's apartment door was directly in front of her, in a tastefully decorated, olive-toned hallway. Ben clutched her planner tightly to her chest and rang the bell. Her heart almost deafened her as the door opened and Cori stood in front of her in shorts and a casual shirt, a cell phone pressed to her ear. She motioned Ben inside.

"I'll just be a minute," she said, covering the phone with her hand. "Feel free to give yourself a tour of the place."

Ben nodded and followed her to the living room. The apartment exceeded her expectations. Light oak hardwood floors were accented with a cherry inlay around the edges. Three large windows afforded a view of Central Park. The room she stood in was furnished in rich brown leather furniture and dark woods, and a massive armoire stood against one wall.

Cori appeared to be doing much more listening than talking to whoever was on the phone, only muttering the occasional sound of agreement. Taking her invitation to look around at face value, Ben wandered back through the foyer and down a hallway. Doors opened on either side and, from a glimpse of tiling at floor level, it looked like a bathroom was straight ahead. She peeked into the bedroom on the left and guessed it to be the master. The décor was simple and more contemporary than the living room. The clean lines of the large bed in the center of the room were accented with a spread of bright blues, white, and muted gray. A matching cherry nightstand and bureau were the only other furnishings in the room.

In the room to the right Cori had set up an easel. Here the floors were covered with drop cloths to protect the wood finish from stray drops of paint. The same view of the park could be seen from the window. Ben wandered around the airy studio, enjoying the atmosphere. She was drawn to the most shadowed wall, where several large canvases stood, protected by drapes. She glanced over her shoulder before lifting a corner exposing a hint of color. Not satisfied, she pulled the cloth back farther. She recognized several of the paintings, but there were several that appeared unfinished. Remembering the canvas in Cori's studio upstate, Ben wondered if these works carried as much pain for her. She made a mental note to ask her about them later in the week.

After carefully covering them once more, Ben made her way back to the living room. She hesitated on the threshold, not wanting Cori to feel she was eavesdropping on her call. Cori lounged on the couch with her feet up on the coffee table. Her white cotton shorts set off long, tan legs. Two buttons of her light blue shirt were open, leaving a vee of smooth skin. Ben suddenly had the urge to press her lips there. *Jesus, I spend entirely too much time thinking about how this woman tastes.*

She must have made a small noise because Cori saw her then and waved her in, gesturing for her to sit in the chair closest to her.

"Yes, Mom, I read the article before it came out." Cori tucked one hand behind her head and looked at Ben pointedly. "I know exactly how persistent the press can be." She grinned when Ben rolled her eyes. "Okay, I'll call you later." She flipped the phone closed and explained, "My mother."

"I gathered."

"She tends to worry too much."

"That's better than not at all."

"I suppose." Cori was confused by the shadow that passed over Ben's expression. "Do you think your mother doesn't worry about you?"

Ben considered her answer. She honestly doubted if her mother gave her any thought. It was not uncommon for several months to pass between their conversations, and even then, it was usually Ben who initiated contact. "I don't know."

"She's your mother. She must."

Ben's dry laugh was humorless. "Not everyone grew up in a fairy tale, Saxton."

Cori was stunned by the rancor in Ben's voice. Certainly, she had not lacked for much when she was growing up, and she hadn't always appreciated what she had. She took for granted that those things would always be there, just as she did her parents' love. They hadn't agreed with her every endeavor, but they had always given her the freedom to go forward and their support whether she succeeded or failed. She could not conceive of a parent not being concerned about their child.

Cori pushed away her musings about her own childhood and focused on the pain that lingered in Ben's eyes. "Tell me," she invited softly.

"We're not here to talk about me," Ben said, but her voice didn't hold much conviction.

Exploiting the hint of uncertainty, Cori reached across the space between them and covered Ben's hand with her own. "Please. You can't make a remark like that about fairy tales and act like it's nothing. If we are going to do this week, it can't be totally one-sided. I want to know something about you too."

She was pleasantly surprised when Ben turned her hand over and laced their fingers. "I guess there were times when we were happy, but except for the early years I can't recall many. I was eight when my brother was diagnosed with leukemia. He was ten. My dad couldn't handle it—his only son with a terminal illness. After a while, when Randy started getting really sick, Dad left."

Ben's mind flashed back to the day she watched her father leave. The image was sharp in her mind, painfully so. He wore a blue striped shirt, the knot of his burgundy tie haphazardly pulled loose. And though she had never been able to put a brand name to his aftershave, she could still recall its musky scent. Randy had been too sick to get out of bed that day; he was already losing his hair from the chemotherapy. Their father had briefly bent over his inert form, pressing his lips to Randy's pale forehead before he headed for the door. He'd brushed a hand lightly over the top of Ben's head as he walked past her. She never saw him again.

"I'm not sure if he was tall."

"What?" Cori asked gently.

Ben's expression was distant and Cori wasn't even sure if she had heard the question. Ben's eyes darted back and forth but her gaze was inward, searching not her line of sight, but her memory of the distant past. "I'm not sure if my father was tall or if I just remember him that way because I was small. After he left, my mother had to work a lot to pay for Randy's hospital bills. Randy and I stayed with our aunt Meg.

"When he—" Her voice cracked and the fingers around Cori's tightened. "His doctors tried everything, but nothing worked. When he died, my mother started working even more. She said it was to pay for his funeral. But I think…"

"What?"

"Well, my brother and I looked a lot alike, and we were both the spitting image of our father—our hair, our coloring. We even have his eyes. After Dad left, then Randy was gone, I think I was just a constant reminder of the two of them. Sometimes I swear she could barely stand to look at me. So she was hardly ever around."

"Oh, sweetie, I'm so sorry." Cori moved to kneel before her, enfolding both of Ben's hands in hers.

Ben shook her head, chasing away the emotions and blinking back tears. "It's okay. I stayed with Aunt Meg a lot. And my cousin Lucy was around the same age, so we sort of grew up together. I had family around me, but—do I think my mother worries about me? I honestly don't know. We rarely speak, and certainly not about anything of substance."

"I always wondered what it would be like to have a brother or a sister," Cori mused.

"It was great. For me at least…poor Randy, he must have hated having his little sister always wanting to tag along, but he never let it show. He was very patient with me."

"You guys didn't argue?"

"Oh, sure we did. But he wouldn't let anyone else give me a hard time." A small smile played at the edge of Ben's lips. "Once, when he and a bunch of his friends were hanging out on the front porch, one of his buddies called me a name. Randy leapt to my defense, and they started yelling at each other. Randy ended up slugging the kid and giving him a black eye."

Cori laughed and shifted to perch back on the edge of the sofa. She kept one of Ben's hands firmly within hers. "Did he get in trouble?"

"My dad pretended to read him the riot act, but I think he was secretly proud of him. The other kid's mother went ballistic and he wasn't allowed to play at our house anymore. I felt so bad that I'd cost Randy a friend that I went to him, crying, and apologized. You know what he said?"

"Hmm?"

"He said, 'That's okay, I didn't like him that much anyway.'" Grinning, Ben glanced up.

Returning her smile, Cori met her eyes for a long moment, then dropped her gaze to their joined hands. She idly stroked her thumb over the top of Ben's.

"It must have been hard for you when he got sick." She pictured an eight-year-old Ben desperately trying to grasp the concept of cancer. She could only imagine what Ben and her family had gone through.

Ben recalled vividly the first time she knew her brother was sick. She knew now that her parents had kept it from her for several weeks. Randy had just begun the treatments and his small body was not dealing well with the radiation and chemotherapy. Ben had been bored one day and had gone in search of her favorite playmate. She found him in the bathroom, pale and shaking, sitting on the floor.

Surprisingly wise for his years, he had immediately seen the fear in her eyes and got to his feet. Taking her hand, he led her into his room. Ben could still feel the cold, sweaty sensation of his flesh against hers. When they were both settled on his bed, he had explained to her straightforwardly what his parents had been unable to bring themselves to tell her. And when she cried, he had simply wrapped his thin arm around her shoulders and waited until her tears had run dry.

"It was the most difficult thing I've ever been through," Ben finally answered.

The knot that had begun forming in Cori's stomach twisted at the agony in her voice. Tears filled Ben's golden eyes, yet she stubbornly refused to let them spill.

❖

For the next thirty minutes, they went over Cori's schedule for the week to follow and compared it to Ben's, deciding when they would get together. Ben was pleased with the outcome. They had a good mix of work and social activities that would give her a well-rounded view of Cori's life for the article. And, she admitted, she was also looking forward to spending time with Cori.

Work out of the way, Cori offered to order a pizza and open a bottle of wine. While waiting for the delivery, they talked casually, meandering from light topics to more serious ones. Their easy conversation seemed in direct contradiction to the sensual energy that seemed to hum between them whenever they were in proximity to each other. Ben had never met anyone who could make her so completely relaxed and yet so instantly turned inside out with barely a word.

When Cori started talking about her high school years, it took some effort for Ben to stay focused on the stories she related in that low, sexy, languid way of hers. Though entertaining, Cori's private school escapades only confirmed that she and Ben could not be more different. Cori had lived a privileged life, and Ben wondered if she had ever realized, or cared, during her teenage years that not everyone had so carefree an existence.

"So this one time when we ditched school, the four of us piled into my car and we headed for the beach." Cori continued her recollections, apparently at ease revealing more about herself than Ben had expected.

"How old were you?" Ben asked.

"A little older than sixteen, I guess, because I hadn't had the car for long."

"Birthday present from Daddy?" Ben asked sarcastically.

"Yeah, actually, it was."

"What kind?"

Cori paused, realizing how telling her answer would be. "It was a Mercedes 500SL."

"Convertible?"

Cori nodded.

"Mmm-hmm…typical."

Cori bristled at the disdain that suffused Ben's words. She'd been judged by strangers all of her life, even more so since her illness became public knowledge, and she was tired of it. "So now you've got me all figured out? You think you know all about me?"

"I didn't mean anything by it." Ben realized that she had reacted to Cori the spoiled rich girl, not Cori the woman she saw now. It wasn't fair to categorize Cori this way, and if she wanted to get to know her better, she needed to guard her reactions a little more. "I'm sorry."

"I know you didn't," Cori said with a sigh. *Shallow, superficial ass.* She wondered if it was foolish to hope Ben would ever see more than that. She settled back into the sofa and changed the subject, launching into another story, this one set in Paris during her art school years.

Ben listened with interest, noting that none of the players in Cori's stories were the same. It seemed that she didn't have many close friends until she returned to the States, and then Gretchen's name was interspersed quite regularly.

When the doorbell rang, Cori got up to answer it. When she disappeared into the foyer, the muted sound of her voice could be heard as she spoke to the delivery person. Ben was glad to have a moment alone to collect her thoughts. It had been almost too easy to lose herself, talking on such a personal level. She never spoke about Randy with anyone except Lucy, yet Cori had tenderly drawn her feelings from her and seemed to have absorbed her pain. Something odd happened to Ben's reserve when she was close to Cori—something that made her want to share things she never had.

Cori returned with a pizza box and two plates. While she served the pizza, Ben refilled their glasses and watched, in amusement, as Cori picked up a slice, folded it in half, and shoved it in her mouth.

"What?" Cori asked before taking another bite.

"There are so many sides to you." Ben laughed.

Cori raised an eyebrow.

"At Gretchen's you were so at ease and socially adept in that crowd. Smooth, I guess. But at your place upstate, and here now… you're just not at all what I expected."

"Mmm…what did you expect?" Cori asked indolently, glancing at her.

"I expected more"—she searched for the proper word—"swagger."

"I can swagger when I need to." Cori chuckled and a small smile graced her lips. "You're not exactly what I expected, either."

"I know. You expected a man," Ben quipped.

"Yeah, sorry about that." But she didn't sound sorry in the least as she raked her eyes purposefully over Ben's body. "There is definitely nothing masculine about you," she teased with a wide grin as her gaze returned to Ben's face.

For a moment Ben basked in the warmth of their shared smile, her body growing increasingly hot under Cori's frank scrutiny. But just as she started thinking about how little effort it would take to close the distance and kiss Cori, Veronica's face flashed in her head.

A heaviness settled around Cori's heart as the smile faded from Ben's face and the intimate moment between them slipped away. "Where did you go?"

"It's late," Ben muttered. She stood and shoved her notebook in her purse. "I'll see you tomorrow. Seven?"

"Yeah." Cori had an appointment the next day with Dr. Franklin. Ben would accompany her to University Hospital in Syracuse. Cori had argued that it wasn't necessary, that certainly *a week in the life* didn't literally mean 24/7. Ben had none too gently reminded her that *she* was calling the shots this time around. Knowing she was arguing in vain, Cori relented, telling Ben they would have to leave early to make the just over four-hour drive.

Cori stood to walk Ben out, but she was barely across the room when the door closed firmly and she heard the ding of the elevator in the hallway. Sighing, she flipped the deadbolt in place and wandered back to the living room. She replayed the evening, dwelling on the pain so vividly reflected in Ben's eyes as she talked about her father's abandonment and her brother's death. Cori had no difficulty picturing a young Ben feeling very much alone as her mother let her down emotionally. Her heart ached for Ben's childhood loss. She was thankful that Ben's aunt and cousin had been there for her.

As she moved around the living room cleaning up the remnants of their dinner, she kept hearing the anguish in Ben's voice as she spoke of her brother. She hadn't said how long Randy was sick before he died, but Cori had gotten the sense that it was a long illness. Ben had probably watched for many months as he got sicker and sicker. Cori had wanted more than anything to take Ben into her arms and comfort her. She wanted Ben to feel safe enough with her to have shed the tears that she had stubbornly held back. *You would damn her to a lifetime of helplessness watching your health deteriorate?*

Cori wasn't sure where that voice came from, but she recognized the wisdom in those words. She was drawn to Ben, of that she had no doubt, but she would keep a professional distance between them in the coming week. She hadn't done too many unselfish things in her life, but this she would do.

CHAPTER THIRTEEN

Dr. Franklin's office was not the luxury suite Ben had expected for a leading neurologist, but a functional set of rooms at University Hospital in Syracuse. Upon arrival they were instructed to have a seat in the small, tastefully decorated waiting room. Cori seemed completely at ease, so Ben wasn't sure why she felt so uncomfortable herself. This was part of their deal. If they didn't explore how Cori was handling her illness in her daily life, there was no point to the follow-up articles. Certainly she shouldn't feel as if she was intruding when Cori had agreed to the arrangement. She knew it was a lie, even as she reduced it in her mind to a business arrangement.

Ben glanced up when a door opened and a nurse instructed, "Ms. Saxton, please come with me."

"You can wait out here," Cori told Ben firmly.

"What?" Annoyed to think she'd driven all this way to sit and read crappy magazines, Ben reminded her, "I'm supposed to be doing a chronicle of your daily life, not just excerpts you choose to share." As soon as she'd spoken, she felt bad. She had always prided herself in knowing the difference between fair investigation and outright invasion of privacy. "I'm sorry," she began, but Cori was already stalking away after the nurse.

Looking back over her shoulder, Cori said, "Come on, if you must."

The nurse showed them to a dressing cubicle and handed over a gown. As she left, Ben started for the gap in the curtains.

"Where are you going?" Cori demanded.

"I'll wait outside to give you some privacy to change."

"That's not necessary. You wanted complete access and that's what you'll get."

Before Ben could respond, Cori tugged her T-shirt over her head, revealing a lean torso and small, firm breasts. Ben could only stare as she proceeded to strip down to her panties and pull on the gown. With an impertinent grin, she turned her back. "A little help?" she prompted, waiting for Ben to tie up her gown.

After Cori had changed, the nurse led them to an examination room. Cori got on the examining table and Ben settled unobtrusively in the chair in one corner and wished she had stayed out front with the potted plants.

Cori shifted uncomfortably on the high bed, tugging the gown that was failing to sufficiently cover her backside.

"Sudden attack of modesty?" Ben asked sarcastically, pretending to flip through the magazine she'd brought with her from the other room.

"I don't think this gown is necessary. It's just a checkup. Plus, this vinyl is cold." Cori winced as her skin came in contact with the offending surface of the exam table once again. "Smart-ass," she added after a beat.

"Tell me again why your doctor is so far away," Ben grumbled, shifting in her seat. They'd just spent the past three hours on I-81. It felt like the longest road ever.

"He comes highly recommended. Besides, I plan on spending a lot more time upstate, so I thought I'd find a neurologist up here in Syracuse."

"Do you think you're actually going to live upstate instead of the city, eventually?" Ben asked, trying to make everyday conversation. She wasn't even sure if Cori answered, she was so distracted by a glimpse of naked breast through the gaping arm of the hospital gown. By all rights, Cori should have looked unappealing in the shapeless blue sack, but the sight of Cori's body as she had unabashedly disrobed was burned in Ben's memory.

Ben shook away her inappropriate thoughts as Dr. Franklin entered the room. He was a thin man with just a fringe of hair ringing his otherwise bald head. A lab coat covered a white shirt and solid navy tie.

Cori made a quick introduction, giving only Ben's name and no explanation as to the reason for her presence. He greeted Ben politely, and if he drew any conclusions about her they did not show on his face.

"How are you feeling?" he asked, shuffling through some papers in the file he was carrying. He pulled a pair of wire-rimmed glasses from his front pocket. His movements seemed careful and deliberate, long fingers carefully settling the glasses on his nose.

"I feel fine." Though Ben was obviously trying to be invisible, keeping her eyes lowered and her hands clasped around a small notepad in her lap, Cori was still aware of her presence, sensing her almost palpably on her skin.

"Your tests look good. You're not experiencing any symptoms?"

Cori shook her head, deciding that the occasional bout of fatigue shouldn't be considered a symptom. "Nothing I can complain about."

"No tremors since the last time we spoke?"

Again she answered in the negative, glancing nervously at Ben. She didn't know why, but she sensed a distance growing between them with each of Dr. Franklin's questions.

"How are you adjusting to the meds? Are the side effects decreasing?"

"Yes. The headaches are fewer and the nausea and chills are pretty much over."

"Have you had any reactions at your injection sites?"

"No. I've been keeping up with the rotation pretty well."

Ben sat silently, trying to absorb the medical terms and specifics of Cori's condition as the two continued to talk about her treatment. She paid particular attention to the things that Cori had not previously explained to her. Every time she heard a word she didn't recognize, she made a note to look it up later.

When Cori had first revealed the nature of her illness, Ben had researched MS extensively on the Internet and had thought she was well versed in the disease, but something about hearing it discussed in the small sterile room made it impossible to feel detached. This was Cori's reality, and no amount of education about the possible progressions of the disease could help anyone predict how or why it would run its course in her body. Ben knew the strange queasiness she felt about that was fear.

"Do you have any questions?" Ben was startled to find Dr. Franklin addressing her.

"No." That was a long way from the truth. She had many questions, but she was no longer able to discern which of them were relevant to her work. She had very personal feelings for Cori, and that could certainly be a problem if she wished to write an objective story.

Some time later, they were seated across from each other at Edy's Place, a little diner just off the interstate that Cori favored when she traveled this route. It was exactly the type of place one expected to find at an interstate exit. A long countertop ran along the back and the stools that were pushed up to it were upholstered in red vinyl, as were the booths that lined the walls. Several tables dotted the open area in the center of the diner, and Ben suspected that if she checked, every one of them would wobble until someone shoved several sugar packets or a strategically folded napkin under them. As soon as they'd walked in they were assailed with the smell of fried food.

Ben had been quiet since they left the hospital, and she now sat silently in her side of the booth, staring at the cracked Formica tabletop.

"What's wrong?" Cori asked casually.

Ben looked up. "Sorry…just lost in thought."

She would have explained herself a little more but they were interrupted by the waitress who sauntered over. After they'd placed their orders and were once again alone, Cori prompted, "So?"

"I guess listening to Dr. Franklin really made things more real," Ben admitted. "I mean, I did the research. I know what MS is. But it was still kind of abstract."

"And now it's real."

"There's a lot to consider, isn't there? And a lot of unknowns."

"Yes, there are. But it's not as bad as it could be. I'm finally getting to a place where I can accept it." *Being around you is helping me with that.* Cori wasn't willing to put voice to this thought but she realized it was true. When she was with Ben, it was easier to remain in the present rather than dwell on what the future might entail.

"Dr. Franklin asked you a lot of questions about the medication you are on now. Is he considering other options for you?"

Cori nodded and waited as their meals were placed in front of them. "I think that's one of the reasons I chose him as my neurologist. He's always aware of the latest research. If the Betaseron isn't working as well as he'd like, there are other drugs we could try to help alleviate the symptoms and reduce the relapses. And he doesn't discount alternative therapies without examining them. For example, he says there has been limited success with hyperbaric oxygen therapy for some symptoms."

Finding her sandwich tastier than she had expected, Ben chewed thoughtfully. "Is there hope for a cure?"

"I guess there's always hope," Cori answered evasively.

Ben wasn't letting her off the hook. If it was only for her article, she could do the research herself. This meant something more. "Knowing you, I'm sure you've looked into this enough to answer more specifically."

"I have." Cori paused to take a sip of her lemonade. "There's extensive research going on, but some of the more promising studies are still in the early stages. I don't know if you've heard about Antigen-specific immunotherapy and stem cell replacement. And there's a lot of buzz about a new drug that could be taken orally instead of by injection."

"Yes, I think I read about that," Ben said, recalling one of the many resources she'd been skimming through online. "It's still in trials, isn't it?"

"Yes, it's several years away from FDA approval."

Trying to sound optimistic, Ben said, "There's really no way to know when a breakthrough might happen."

"By the time it does, it could be too late to do me much good."

Cori didn't seem bitter, only resigned. "I have to be realistic, and plan accordingly."

"So when you said you plan on spending a lot more time upstate, how much time exactly do you mean?" Ben returned to the question she'd asked in Dr. Franklin's office earlier. She felt barren at the thought that they could live miles apart in the near future.

"I need to make some changes in my life," Cori said. "There's really no reason for me to stay in the city. My place in Ogdensburg has everything I could want."

"Well, it is beautiful up there," Ben agreed, her heart sinking.

Cori picked up the check their waitress had laid on the table and pulled her wallet out of her back pocket.

"Hey, give me that." Ben protested. "It's a business lunch. We'll make Mitch pay for it." She took the check and placed her credit card in the folder. "Don't you think you'll miss your lifestyle?"

"What do you mean?"

Ben searched for the words to be tactful and then decided it was futile. "The pool of available lesbians is much smaller upstate."

"Who are we kidding, Ben? I've never limited myself to the *available* ones." Cori gave a self-deprecating chuckle. "I guess that's one of things that will have to change. I think I can live without sex."

Ben couldn't stop the disbelieving look before it flew across her face.

"I can!" Cori insisted.

CHAPTER FOURTEEN

I can't believe I let you talk me into this," Lucy grumbled, bending over to tie her shoe.

They stood together just inside Central Park. The early morning sun was beginning to burn off the previous night's dew. The peaceful chirping of the birds competed with the ever-present sounds of the city.

"It'll be good for us. I should get in shape." Needing to work off some energy, Ben had called Lucy and convinced her that a walk would be nice. When Lucy hesitated, Ben insisted, saying that they hadn't had much time to spend together lately and she missed her. Lucy couldn't argue with that but she made her feelings about exercise very clear.

"Just because you want to look good so you can get in Cori's pants doesn't mean my fat ass has to sweat."

Ben snorted. Lucy was naturally shapely in all the right places, but she would never be called fat. "I am not trying to get in Cori's pants," she protested.

"Then you're crazy." Lucy gave her a salacious grin. "Mind if I have a go at her?"

When Ben's only response was a dark glare, Lucy laughed.

"Come on." Ben pulled Lucy along the path. "I only have an hour before I have to meet her."

As they passed through a treed area, the sunlight poked through in a random dappled pattern and reached down to touch the ground. They walked in silence for a while, settling into a brisk pace.

"Are you still upset about the blonde?" Lucy broke the silence tentatively.

"No," Ben answered too quickly. "Maybe. Yes. But I don't have any right to be. She can sleep with whomever she chooses."

"But it bothers you," Lucy gently pointed out that Ben was not nearly as neutral as she wanted to be.

"Yeah," Ben admitted with a sigh.

"But you can see why she had another fling, can't you?"

"Because she's a player and she'll never change." Ben fell in behind Lucy, walking briefly in single file as they met a woman pushing a stroller.

"Come on, Ben. MS is a big deal. Her life is changing beyond her control, and your article just basically outed her to the whole world. Maybe she had something to prove."

"Please tell me you're not going to take her side." Ben caught up with her again. "She agreed to the article."

"I'm taking whatever side will result in you being happy. All I'm saying is, think carefully before you let anything happen with her. Cori is the one-night stand type, but you're not."

"What's that supposed to mean?"

"You get emotionally involved. From all accounts, she doesn't. She has no depth. I don't think you need someone like that messing with your head."

Ben walked on in silence, pondering Lucy's observation. Once again she was struck by the discrepancies between the woman people thought Cori was and the one Ben was getting to know. Cori might not have been emotionally involved with her previous sexual partners, but Ben didn't think she lacked the ability.

No depth. She recalled the warmth between Cori and Henry as well as the closeness she had witnessed with Gretchen. Cori was capable of depth, of that Ben was certain.

"You don't have to have sex with someone to be emotionally involved." The words were out before Ben realized just how much they revealed. Though she was resolutely staring straight ahead she could feel Lucy's eyes on her.

"Oh, no, Ben. No."

"What?"

"You're falling for her," Lucy accused.

Ben considered denying it, but Lucy would see right through her anyway. When Ben walked on silently, Lucy grabbed her arm, forcing them both to a stop.

"Ben? What are you doing?"

"I can't help it, Luce. She's not like the person you see in the tabloids."

"That's what they all say."

"She's not," Ben insisted quietly. "She *is* exciting and sexy. But she's also sweet and kind. And, I don't know, sometimes when she looks at me it's as if there is no one else in the world."

"And you're sure it's not just an act?"

They were in the middle of the path and the foot traffic was picking up. Several people gave them annoyed looks as they were forced to go around them. Ben tugged Lucy to a nearby bench off the path.

"She's vulnerable in ways that I'm not even sure that she is aware of, otherwise I'm sure she would hide it."

"Why her? I mean, you're a good-looking woman and there are plenty of attractive, available, *healthy* women out there."

"Lucy."

Concern clouded her cousin's eyes. "You know what I mean, don't tell me you haven't thought about it."

"Okay. I know she has—health concerns. But I've dealt with that before."

"My point exactly." Lucy slid closer and took Ben's hand in hers. Ben recognized the attempt to soften the impact of her words. "Don't you remember how hard that was?"

"Of course I do. Do you think I could forget?" Ben's heart ached as Randy's face swam into focus. Against her will, hot tears sprang into her eyes.

"I'm sorry. I'm not trying to upset you." Lucy squeezed her hand.

Ben swiped the back of her hand across her eyes. "It's okay. But enough time has passed that I also remember the good times. I wouldn't wish those times away just to have missed the pain."

"I know."

"And if it was in the cards for me to be involved with Cori, I wouldn't avoid it just because there may be hard times." Ben fell silent immediately, shocked by her own admission.

But she'd spoken the truth. Cori's uncertain future scared her, but not enough to drive her away. The very thought of being with her sent a shiver of anticipation down her spine. A blush crept up her neck, warming her skin. She thought about the kiss they had shared and the feeling of being curled up on the sofa talking with Cori while a storm raged just outside. She wanted more than that. It was probably impossible, but if the opportunity arose Ben was no longer sure she would be able to resist.

"I love you, Ben, and I just want you to think about what you would be getting into," Lucy said. "You would be signing up for a lifetime of—"

Ben cut her off quickly. "Whoa, slow down there. I didn't say I was signing up for a lifetime of anything. Besides, we've spent a lot of time together in the past few days, and I don't have the impression that Cori's interested in getting involved with me."

Lucy regarded her skeptically. "Whatever you say."

❖

An hour later, her conversation with Lucy still running through her head, Ben leaned against the wall of the elevator in Cori's building. She was still evaluating her feelings. There really was no denying that she was attracted to Cori, and she was fairly certain it was mutual. But she didn't know if Cori wanted a relationship, and Ben didn't think she could accept anything less.

As the elevator doors opened on Cori's floor, Ben pushed aside her thoughts. There would be time for introspection later. She crossed the hall and pressed the doorbell, willing her heartbeat to remain steady. By now, she should be used to seeing Cori. It was silly to overreact the way she did.

Cori opened the door in the midst of buttoning her shirt. Her slightly damp hair stood on end where she had apparently been running her fingers through it. The lavender button-down shirt was crisply starched and showed a tantalizing strip of skin just before she drew it closed.

"I'll be ready in a minute." She turned away, shoving her shirttails into the waistband of her jeans and leaving Ben to follow her.

"So what's on the agenda for today?" Ben settled on the sofa as Cori wandered down the hall.

"Lunch with Gretchen," Cori called through the open door of her bedroom. "Then shopping."

When she returned to the living room she had added a brown leather belt with an oversized buckle and was clipping her cell phone onto it. She glanced up at Ben, one eyebrow cocked enticingly. "Ready?"

"Yes." Ben jumped up and moved past her, careful to avoid contact. She pushed the elevator button and forced herself not to turn around and stare as Cori locked up.

❖

They stepped inside the trendy restaurant. The décor was dominated by dark wood and subdued burgundy wallpaper that would have substantially darkened the interior had it not been for the large windows that lined the front of the space, letting in sufficient natural light.

A wiry man rushed over to greet them. "Ms. Saxton, Ms. Mills has already been seated. Please, this way."

Cori waited for Ben to precede her and then stepped close behind, laying a hand lightly against the small of her back. Realizing it was probably an automatic gesture didn't keep Ben's heartbeat from accelerating.

When they reached the table tucked discreetly in a rear corner of the room, the maître d' seated them both.

"Ben, it's good to see you again." Gretchen smiled in greeting.

"Yes, you too."

Once again Ben was struck by how polished and together

Gretchen looked. Today she wore a striped silk blouse open at the neck to reveal a strand of pearls. Her dark hair was twisted back and pinned behind her head. How did the woman look utterly gorgeous and make it appear effortless? Ben had changed her own clothes three times and still felt dowdy next to her.

The waiter approached and they each ordered the house special, a lightly glazed chicken breast and a watercress salad. Ben sipped her iced tea and listened quietly as Cori and Gretchen talked business. She was impressed with Gretchen's thoroughness and her ability to keep Cori on track. She had no doubt that Cori could handle the business end of her career if she needed to. However, having Gretchen there to do it gave her a degree of freedom that surely helped her creativity. There was obviously an enormous amount of trust between the two women as well as an easy friendship.

"How rude of us to exclude you, Ben. I'm sorry," Gretchen said smoothly as their meals arrived.

"It's quite all right, thank you. Cori is supposed to be carrying on with daily life as if I'm not here," Ben replied politely.

"Well, we can hardly ignore the fact that you're here." Gretchen smiled.

Cori's eyes narrowed. Gretchen's smile was just a tad too friendly for her liking.

"Is Mitchell driving you crazy about this article?" Gretchen asked, lifting the linen napkin from her lap and dabbing the corners of her mouth carefully.

"He's—ah—" Ben searched for a way to politely express Mitchell's involvement.

Gretchen laughed. "It's okay. Mitchell and I have traveled in the same circles professionally for years, I know how he can be."

"He likes to see how far he can push me before I push back. It's a game we play," Ben explained.

"Yes, well, from what I understand there aren't too many people working at that magazine of his who will push back. You're certainly in the minority. But I too have found Mitchell responds well to a firm hand." She paused to sip her Chardonnay, then asked, "Are you seeing anyone, Ben?"

Cori's head snapped around in Gretchen's direction.

"Um." Ben dropped her fork onto her plate. "No, I'm not."

"Really? Because I have a friend, she owns a gallery downtown, and you two might hit it off."

"Gretchen," Cori said sharply.

"What? I'm just saying if she's not seeing anyone they might get along."

"Actually, thank you, but I'm working a lot right now and I don't have much time for dating." Between Cori's murderous gaze and Gretchen's guileless expression, Ben did not know which way to look, so she stared down at her plate. Her cheeks were hot.

"Well, if you change your mind," Gretchen offered with a shrug.

"I'll let you know," Ben said.

Cori watched the exchange in disbelief, irritated by the stab of jealousy she felt. The thought of Ben going out with someone else affected her far more than it should. So did Gretchen's interference. Unsettled, she turned her attention back to her salad and quietly picked through her meal while Gretchen and Ben carried on casual conversation. They seemed to be getting along as if they'd known each other for years.

When Ben excused herself to go to the restroom, Cori rounded on her friend. "What are you doing?"

"What?" Gretchen feigned innocence.

"Trying to fix her up. Was that necessary? And were you flirting with her?"

"What if I were? You don't want her."

"When did I say that?"

"Oh, please. If you really wanted her it would already have happened and she would be old news by now." The challenging spark in Gretchen's eyes drew exactly the response it always did.

Cori's temper flared. "Are you telling me that if I don't act soon, you are going to fix her up with someone else? Or," she could hardly keep her voice even, "nail her yourself?"

"Cori," Gretchen gave her a long-suffering smile, "what I'm telling you is very simple. If you two aren't going to get over yourselves and realize you want each other so much that anyone within twenty feet can see it, then eventually she's going to have to date someone else. Why shouldn't I...er...lubricate that process?"

"So that means you have to help her along, right in front of me?" Cori hissed softly. "Damn it, Gretchen."

"I was just trying to—"

"*Jesus Christ,* is the whole world conspiring against me right now?"

"Cori—"

"Just forget it." Cori pushed her hand through her hair, struggling to tamp down her anger. She knew her feelings were irrational—after all, she had already decided that she was not going to act on her desires. Gretchen had every right to treat Ben as an attractive, available single, and there was nothing Cori could do about it. In fact, she should be thanking her. Ben deserved to find happiness with someone. Preferably a very plain woman with no personality who would bore her to tears. She glared at Gretchen, then recalled part of her little speech. *If you two aren't going to get over yourselves and realize you want each other...*

"Do you really think Ben wants me?"

Gretchen groaned. In a sarcastic tone, she said, "No, I think she's really after your car and your money."

"Very funny." And it was. For once in her life, Cori knew for a fact that her background would buy her nothing. If Ben wanted her, it would not be because she drove a Jag and was heiress to a mountain of money.

"I thought so too." Gretchen smiled.

Cori gave her a small shove. "Why are you always a jump ahead of me?"

"Because it's my job to be."

When Ben returned, Cori immediately snatched up the check and deposited several bills on the table. "Are you ready?" she asked, standing.

"Sure." Ben only had a chance to exchange a polite farewell with Gretchen before Cori clamped a hand on her arm and steered her away. "Where are we going?" she asked as they left the restaurant.

"A little shopping," Cori replied in an odd tone. "That's what shallow, superficial asses like me do when we want something we can't have."

❖

"See anything you like?" Cori asked, too close for comfort.

Ben jumped. "Not really." She'd never been in a boutique where one outfit cost more than she made in a month.

Cori lifted an exquisitely cut pantsuit in a soft gray pinstripe. "This would look good on you."

Ben gave a noncommittal shrug. "It's not something I would buy."

She wished they could leave. Cori's barb as they left the restaurant had found its mark, and she felt hurt to be reminded of her own rush to judgment. She'd thought they had let go of their preconceptions enough to move forward. Apparently not. She moved away from Cori, wandering among the stylishly displayed racks of clothing. Everything she looked at was wildly out of her price range.

Cori watched as Ben moved through the store, absently fingering the sleeves of several garments. She had seen the naked appreciation in her eyes as she studied the gray suit. Ben had good taste, and it would fit her beautifully. She glanced at the suit again and speculated on Ben's size. Probably a ten. She could see Ben was restless, obviously bored with fashion shopping.

"Something wrong?" Cori asked, following her around a stand of cashmere sweaters.

"No. I'm just realizing how different our lives really are." Ben glanced pointedly at the pile of garments draped over Cori's arm.

"Well, I'll agree that we grew up under different circumstances, but I think now—"

"Need I remind you that your car costs more than I make in a year?" Ben interrupted. "Hell, I wouldn't even be able to guess how many weeks' salary it would cost me to buy one of your paintings."

"Don't buy one. I'll give you one."

Ben gave Cori a withering look before turning to pretend disinterest in another rack of temptingly lovely clothing she couldn't afford. She could feel an underlying tension in Cori, and every comment she made seemed to have an edge to it. Ben stole a quick glance at her and was relieved to see that she was at the counter, speaking to the clerk.

Ben gave her time to finish paying for her purchases before joining her.

"We'll have your packages delivered, Ms. Saxton," the clerk assured her.

The pleasant veneer Cori had affected when dealing with the clerk dissolved as they stepped onto the street. To Ben's dismay, Cori was back to her sullen self.

❖

If Cori had hoped to see Ben show up for dinner the next evening in the pinstripe suit, she was disappointed.

"I can't accept it," Ben insisted as soon as she walked into the apartment. She was wearing a light blue silk blouse and black slacks. Nice, but a snub.

"Well, I'm not taking it back." Cori calmly poured wine and wondered how she was supposed to have handled this. What was wrong with her wanting to give Ben a gift? It wasn't jewelry.

"It's too much," Ben said.

"It's not like I don't have the money." Cori had never met a woman who had refused to have money spent on her. Trying to explain that the gesture was no big deal, she said, "It's nothing to me. I spend more on getting my house cleaned."

Ben stared at her. There was an edge to Cori's tone that she didn't much care for. "That's not really the point. I don't make a habit of accepting expensive gifts from my interview subjects."

Ben actually seemed insulted. Cori supposed it was some silly issue of hurt pride and she felt patronized, or whatever. "It wasn't expensive," she reiterated.

"Not for you, perhaps. But I don't spend thousands on my wardrobe."

"Keep the damn suit, return it and keep the money, give it to a fucking homeless person, I don't care. I'm not taking it back," Cori snapped.

Ben didn't bring it up again, and they had both acted as if it had never happened as they dined together. Their week was fast coming to an end and Cori didn't want to conclude it on a sour note. She had grown used to Ben's presence, far too used to it. Ben had spent several hours each day with her, rotating between mornings, afternoons, and evenings so she would get a well-rounded idea of Cori's daily life.

However, at some point, at least for Cori, the week had become less about how she spent her days and more about enjoying the time shared with Ben. In another day's time, Ben would be going back to her life and Cori would be faced with the void left by her departure. She already knew she was going to miss Ben, but in her usual fashion she decided to focus only on the present. The future could take care of itself.

So she'd planned a quiet evening in. It turned out that Ben did like fettuccini Alfredo, and Cori had tossed in some grilled chicken as well. She served it with fresh grated parmesan and a nice Merlot.

After arranging plates on the dining-room table and lighting candles, Cori declared dinner ready. She pulled out Ben's chair and waited for her to be seated. She sat across from her and waited while Ben took a bite.

"Once again, you've surprised me," Ben commented. She savored a bite of the tender chicken and rich sauce.

"How's that?"

"I didn't expect you to be such a good cook. The steaks on the grill were one thing, but this is quite another. I figured expensive restaurants were more your style."

"While I will concede a reservation at an exclusive place seems to impress," Cori sipped her wine, "there's something to be said for an intimate dinner in private."

Ben smiled. "Yes, there is. Do you do this often?"

"Not really." *You're the first.* "I don't bring many women here."

"Ah, yes, easier to leave if you're at their place." It was said without a trace of bitterness.

And instead of reacting defensively, Cori simply acknowledged the truth of her statement with a shrug. "More wine?" she asked as they finished their meal.

When Ben lifted her glass, Cori refilled it. The candlelight and wine were doing the trick, and when Cori gave her that familiar smoldering look, Ben wanted to believe it was only for her. "You're certainly very good at this."

"I'm better than you think," Cori drawled. Her eyes lingered on Ben's mouth.

"Well, that remains to be seen." The warmth of Cori's gaze was intoxicating and Ben found herself wanting to give in to it. Sitting there in Cori's dining room, just a few feet from her bedroom, she allowed herself to wonder just what Cori had in mind. She'd been sweetly sexy and attentive all evening, and Ben had the impression it was not their meal that brought the fire into her eyes.

"Would you care for some dessert?" Cori asked.

"I really shouldn't." *But, oh God, do I want to.* Ben was overwhelmed by the feeling that they were building toward something she was not ready for. She did not want to be simply another woman seduced by Cori Saxton. She wanted more. *Too much more.* "In fact, it's late. I'd better be going."

"It's early," Cori argued as Ben rose from the table.

"Really, I should go. Dinner was delicious." Ben headed for the door and Cori followed. "Are you still planning to go to the gym tomorrow morning?"

"Yes." Cori drew close as they paused in the foyer. She touched Ben's arm lightly. "I enjoyed having dinner with you."

Ben swayed toward her, the gentle touch and sincere words were even more charming than the arrogant sexuality Cori usually displayed. And once again she found herself fighting the urge to kiss her. The need to touch her was too strong, though. Ben stepped closer and embraced her, her face against Cori's neck.

"Thank you for dinner," she murmured.

For a split second, it seemed that Cori would not let her leave, but she fell back a pace as Ben opened the door.

Much later that night, as she lay in bed staring at the closet where the suit hung, Ben thought about something her mother occasionally said. *Nothing like sleeping in your own bed.* Unless that bed was suddenly terribly lonely. She rolled over and closed her eyes. Cori's seductive gaze played across her closed eyelids as she drifted off to sleep.

CHAPTER FIFTEEN

Ben signed her name in the next available line on the clipboard and handed it back to the impressively muscled man on the other side of the counter. She could count on one hand the number of times she had been in a gym in the past year. Luckily, she was blessed with a slightly better than average metabolism that kept her at an even weight as long as she watched what she ate most of the time.

Cori routinely worked out at George's Gym not far from her apartment and had arranged for Ben to be admitted with her as a guest. This was not one of those chain establishments with their expensive cardio equipment that required nothing more of a person than to perch upon it. The only treadmill in the place was tucked in one corner. The rest of the room was divided in half, one side devoted to free weights and the other to machines. At midday, the room was nearly empty.

Ben found Cori amidst the free weights. She stumbled to a stop a few feet from her. Cori bent over, her back to Ben, and smoothly touched her palms to the floor, stretching. *My, but she's flexible.* Cori's nylon shorts rode up slightly, revealing a length of thigh. Smooth, tan muscles elongated and then contracted as Cori straightened. Ben's mouth went dry. Their eyes met in the mirror that covered one wall and Ben was certain Cori could read the lust in hers. Time stopped as their gazes locked. Ben was the first to break eye contact.

"So, what's first?" she asked with false enthusiasm and rubbed her hands together.

"You should stretch so you don't pull anything." Cori raised her arms over her head and leaned to the side.

"Right, always a good idea to stretch," Ben mumbled to herself. "Wouldn't want to hurt myself." Cori's limber body sapped her strength. She could imagine what would happen if she tried to lift anything over a pound; she would probably drop it on her foot.

"Are you talking to yourself?" Cori grinned, enjoying Ben's distracted state a bit too much. She had purposely lingered longer than necessary when she bent over to stretch and she'd been rewarded by a flash of need in Ben's eyes. Her body reacted immediately. Heat, liquid and molten, suffused her limbs and pooled between her thighs.

"Yep. So," Ben began while halfheartedly lunging forward to stretch her legs, "do you come here often?"

Cori raised an eyebrow. "Why, Ben, is that a line? Are you trying to pick me up?"

"I—uh." Normally she would be more composed, but considering the path her thoughts had been taking she had to fight to keep from blurting out, *Yes, yes I am. I want to take you home and do unspeakable things to your body.* Jesus, where did that come from?

Cori watched in amusement as arousal and then shock slid across Ben's face. She liked being able to read her expressions so easily and wondered if Ben knew how much her face gave her away.

"Actually, I go through cycles when I slack off on working out. But I always feel better when I'm more disciplined and get here regularly," Cori explained, letting Ben off the hook. "I want to bench-press first. Will you spot me?"

When Ben nodded, Cori led her over to the bench and began sliding weights onto one end of the bar.

"This won't be too much?" Ben asked as she slid enough weight on the bar to balance out the side Cori was loading up. In total, it was far more than Ben could've handled.

"I'm not an invalid yet," Cori retorted sharply as she dropped down onto the bench and slid under the bar.

"I didn't—I didn't think you were." Ben moved to stand behind the bar, spotting Cori as she lifted and then lowered the weight carefully to her chest. Her biceps were tight with the controlled effort, and cords of muscle stood out on her forearms. As she finished a set of reps, a fine sheen of sweat broke out on her brow.

Exhaling, she pushed the weight back up and paused. "Damn it," she muttered under her breath. She was snapping at everyone lately and she didn't know what was wrong with her. "I'm sorry. I don't know why I'm so on edge lately. It's not your fault."

Avoiding eye contact, Ben nodded silently, her hands hovering close enough to the bar to catch it if needed. Cori had been noticeably on edge. Though overall they were having a pleasant week, Ben had witnessed several bouts of short temper on Cori's part that she had tried unsuccessfully to hide.

"Anyway," Cori said. "I've done something about it. Straight after this we are going to the day spa for a massage. I booked a full-body session for both of us. My treat."

❖

Ben stepped into the sauna behind Cori with a towel clutched tightly around her. She'd left her robe on the hook outside the door. Though she and Cori were the only two occupants, she couldn't bring herself to drop the towel. When Cori settled on a bench, Ben chose the one perpendicular to her. The warm mist enveloped her, bringing a flush to her skin.

"God, I needed this," Cori moaned, tilting her head back against the wall and closing her eyes. When she planted one foot on the bench and raised her knee, her towel dropped aside, baring a length of thigh. "You know what I mean?"

"Ah—yes. Yes, I do." Ben cleared her throat in an attempt to cover the roughness of her voice. Through the steam she watched a bead of sweat trace over Cori's cheek, disappearing for a moment only to reappear on her neck. It pooled in the hollow where her collarbones met. "Cori?"

"Yeah."

"The woman at the desk said a spa treatment *for two...*"

"Oh, yeah. They have this package where you go through

the whole thing together. You know, massages in the same room." Cori opened her eyes to challenge Ben with a frank stare. "Is that a problem?"

"No. No problem." Closing her own eyes seemed to be the only way Ben could relax. Her body was reacting to the sight of Cori and coiling more tightly. Even when she couldn't see her, she could sense her nearness.

"I really am sorry I snapped at you earlier. I'm just a little touchy about my health right now," Cori said suddenly a few moments later.

"It's okay. I understand."

"I just didn't want you to think it was personal. Since today was our last day together. I wanted you to be able to enjoy being pampered, with no hard feelings between us."

The realization that the spa day had been planned as much for her benefit as for Cori's sparked a warmth within her.

"Are you?" Cori prompted. "Enjoying this?"

Ben traced her eyes over Cori's body covered only in a towel, the swell of her breasts evident beneath it. When her gaze returned to Cori's face, she found awareness burning just as brightly there.

"Yes." Ben was saved from commenting further when an attendant came to retrieve them for their massage.

They were led into a room large enough to accommodate two massage tables draped with sheets. Aromatherapy candles dispersed the relaxing scent of lavender and sage, and a sideboard along one wall held an array of lotions and oils.

"Get comfortable, ladies. Your masseuses will be with you shortly," the woman instructed before leaving them alone.

Cori immediately took off her robe and slipped beneath the sheet, but not before Ben got a glimpse of her strong back and firm buttocks. While Cori was still getting settled, Ben hurriedly did the same, dragging the sheet over her body as she stretched out on her stomach.

A moment later the door opened and two women entered. They introduced themselves and confirmed Cori's arrangements for a relaxing full-body massage.

Warm hands pulled the sheet from Cori's back and folded it low over her hips. She sighed as lightly scented oil was rubbed into her back. She really had needed this; it had been far too long since she treated herself. And having Ben close by made it even better. The hum of arousal between them seemed to shimmer in the air, and Cori wouldn't have been surprised if the other two women in the room could feel it. She groaned when her masseuse hit a particularly tight spot in her shoulder.

"You're all knotted up here," the woman murmured, applying firmer pressure and working the muscles.

"That's so good," Cori sighed as she felt the knot loosen.

She looked over at Ben. Her face was pressed into the opening in the table. Cori bit back a moan when her masseuse folded back the sheet to bare Ben's legs. The curve of her ass was just visible where it met her thighs.

Ben turned her head sideways on her folded arm and glanced across the few feet that separated them to find Cori staring at her. Her mind as languid as her muscles, Ben could only gaze back. She had no defenses for the clear intentions burning in Cori's eyes. And in that moment it was Cori's hand that moved over her, Cori's fingers that kneaded the backs of her thighs. Cori's mouth that she wanted— *Jesus*. She jerked her eyes away and buried her face back in the cushioned head support. She was fully aroused and wet, and a stranger's fingers were far too close to discovering it.

For the rest of the massage, she kept her eyes averted, but there was no way she could shut out the soft sighs that drifted from the other table. When they were finished the masseuses left the room, instructing them to take the time they needed before leaving. They lay there in silence for a few minutes until Ben shifted off her table and reached quickly for her robe. She didn't look at Cori as they made their way back to the dressing room.

When Cori reached into the attached cubicle and turned a faucet, Ben said, "What are you doing?"

"I'm going to shower before I get dressed. There's plenty of room in here for you to join me."

Ben stared at her as she loosened the belt of her robe and

prepared to step inside. A shower. With Cori. There was no way she could go in there and pretend that the entire massage had not just been foreplay. "You know—I'm not feeling so well. I think I'll just shower at home."

"Are you okay?" Cori stepped closer, concern in her voice.

"Yeah. Yes, I'm fine. The massage was wonderful. I'm just a little light-headed."

"Okay, let's get you home, then." Cori turned off the shower and began pulling on her clothes.

As far as Ben was concerned, she could not dress fast enough. Ben just wanted to get out of there. Cori's thoughtful gift had been supposed to relax her, but all it had done was inflame her already overactive libido.

"Stay for a glass of wine," Cori urged as she unlocked the door to her apartment and stepped inside.

"I really need to go home and take a shower," Ben said. *A cold shower.*

She could not even look at Cori; she was afraid that if she did, she would not be able to resist her. She wanted to believe the desire she had seen during their massage was for her, personally, but common sense told her otherwise. Cori was a sexual being and Ben could be any desirable woman. For Cori, sex was just sex; she'd made that very clear.

"Please, don't rush away," Cori begged softly. "I would really like your company."

Fool, Ben thought, but relented anyway. "One glass, then I have to go."

She followed Cori into the living room and settled uneasily on the couch while Cori headed for the kitchen.

Cori returned carrying two glasses of a deep red wine. She handed one to Ben before sitting at the other end of the sofa. She raised her glass in a toast. "To us. We got through a whole week together and we're still talking."

Ben tried to seem enthusiastic and impersonal in her agreement. "Yes, to a job well done. I hope you'll like my articles."

"I'll be very interested to see how you describe today," Cori said blandly.

Ben gulped down most of her wine as she tried to think of a reply. "Let's stop doing this."

"Why?" Cori leaned her head against the back of the couch, revealing an expanse of throat that drew Ben's eyes. "I'm having fun. I like flirting with you."

"You like flirting with any attractive woman."

"That's true," Cori conceded with a self-effacing sigh. "Are you saying you don't want to be one of many?"

"I suppose I am," Ben replied.

"Then don't be." Cori took Ben's glass from her unresisting fingers and placed it on the low coffee table in front of the couch. Taking this as an invitation to leave, Ben tried to stand, but Cori's hand prevented her. "Where are you going?"

"Home. This past week has been great, spending time with you—but it has also been agonizingly frustrating." The words were out before Ben could stop them. She hadn't realized how much the wine had dulled her inhibitions. She sank back against the soft cushions and mumbled, "Ah—never mind."

"You can't leave it there." Cori withdrew her hand leaving Ben's arm tingling. "Why has it been frustrating?"

Ben's mind raced for a suitable alternative to the truth. Finally she realized she would just have to take a leap. "I can't stop thinking about *you*, even when I don't want to. That kiss. I—" She broke off, realizing she was dangerously close to admitting she fantasized about Cori.

"I think about that kiss too," Cori said. "It's a pity we stopped there."

"I'm thankful we did," Ben said honestly. "Like I said, I don't do one-night stands."

"What do you do?" Cori asked and, again, her tone had an edge. "Fall in love and get married? You seem very single for someone who has *real* relationships."

Ben had the impression she was being provoked deliberately. "I'm single because I don't have relationships unless I really care about someone. The right kind of woman isn't that easy to find."

"Really?" Cori's eyes drew Ben's. Very softly, she said, "It's funny…I feel exactly the same way. I just console myself differently." Before Ben could speak again, she said, "I have something to tell you."

Ben wasn't sure that she wanted to hear it. With every word, with every glance, Cori was undoing her, and she knew if she didn't leave soon she would do or say something she would regret. Cautiously, she prompted, "I'm listening."

"You are the only woman I have ever invited to stay upstate… the only person who has ever been inside that studio. You're not one of many. I just want you to know that."

The eyes Ben met were bright with tears, and something else. Ben didn't think she was imagining the yearning in their depths. Confused, she scooted along the sofa until their thighs were almost touching. "Cori, what are you saying?"

When Cori remained silent, Ben reached up and traced a fingertip down the side of her neck. Cori sucked in her breath and held perfectly still. Ben framed her face gently, laying her palms alongside Cori's cheeks. She lightly traced the indent in Cori's chin and brushed her fingers over the angles of Cori's face—brows—cheekbones—jawline. *Slowly.* It was an attempt to memorize Cori's face.

Cori couldn't tear her eyes from Ben's. *Jesus, it's too much.* The tenderness she found there was almost unbearable. "I can't get you out of my head," she confessed hoarsely, seconds before Ben's mouth covered hers. It threatened to be the last coherent thought she ever had. The feel of Ben's lips yielding to hers consumed her. The taste and texture of Ben's tongue ingrained itself in her senses.

"What have you been thinking about?" Ben pulled back only far enough to get the words out, her lips still lightly rubbing against Cori's as she spoke.

"This. I think about this." *And so much more.*

"What else?" Ben encouraged. She moved her mouth to Cori's neck tasting the slight saltiness of her skin.

I could lose myself in her. Everything else would disappear. Cori froze. "I—uh—I need a shower. Excuse me."

Ben drew a sharp, uneven breath as Cori sprang from the couch and practically ran from the room.

Somehow Cori made it into her bathroom and leaned against the closed door, breathing hard. She stripped off her clothes and dropped them on the floor. Stepping into the stall, she twisted the knob all the way to cold and gasped as the icy spray hit her. Within seconds, her racing blood had cooled.

She leaned against the shower wall, panting. *Everything else would disappear.* She had been seconds away from forgetting everything except the way Ben felt against her. She hadn't wanted to think about what she would be taking from Ben, but it had shoved its way into her mind. Since she'd already decided that subjecting Ben to a relationship with her would be unfair, this encounter would be reduced to one night. She had nothing more than that to offer Ben.

Ben paced outside the bathroom door. *I should leave, just go home.* But she had seen the heat in Cori's eyes. She had felt the energy arcing between them. Then Cori had fled. *I didn't imagine it. She wants me as much as I want her.* Cori was letting her head get in the way. *You're not one of many.* Her decision made, Ben tried the knob and found the door unlocked. She slipped quietly inside the bathroom.

When the stall door opened behind her, Cori turned. She stared as Ben paused before stepping inside. *God, she's beautiful.* She couldn't keep her gaze from straying over Ben's body. She was all luscious curves, from her rose-tipped breasts to her gently flaring hips. She had just spent several minutes talking herself out of her lust for Ben. In seconds her efforts were undone. Her heart pounded in her ears and her skin flushed hot despite the cold water.

Cori couldn't tear her eyes away from Ben's body. It couldn't be considered rude to stare at a woman after she had walked nude into the shower with her, could it? Ben advanced, stopping just inches from her.

"I think we need some hot water here." She reached around Cori and turned the faucet. "I'm not really in the mood for a cold shower."

Ben enjoyed seeing Cori flustered. Smiling, she pressed closer until they both stood under the spray. Her breasts brushed Cori's. Though she was fairly certain this little scene would not make it into her articles, she mentally recorded it all the same. No matter what happened, she would have this, she thought. It was better than nothing at all.

"Turn around." Without waiting for Cori to move, Ben took her by the shoulders and turned her firmly. She squeezed some shampoo into her hand and buried her fingers in Cori's hair. Cori moaned just loudly enough to be heard over the pounding spray as Ben's fingers massaged her scalp. When she was finished lathering, Ben twisted her fingers into Cori's hair and pulled her head back. "Rinse," she ordered.

"Hey."

"What? You want gentle?" Ben teased. She lightened her touch, stroking Cori's hair until all the shampoo was out. She grazed her fingertips lightly over Cori's shoulders. "I can do gentle."

"Ben." Cori grasped Ben's waist. "I can't think with you doing that."

"I can do whatever you want, baby," Ben purred with a sudden burst of bravado. She wrapped her arms around Cori, pressing closer, and rubbed soapy hands over Cori's back.

"God, Ben."

"Hmm?" Ben grasped Cori's ass in her slippery hands.

"Don't stop." Any protest melted away when Ben tilted her hips and moved against her.

"Oh, I have no intention of stopping." Applying a little more pressure, Ben ran her fingernails up Cori's back and over her shoulder blades.

Cori shivered. She could absolutely melt under those fingers. When Ben's nails raked once more along the length of her back, her senses skyrocketed and her body vibrated with the need to have Ben beneath her. She desperately struggled to regain her composure before she embarrassed herself.

"Mmm, hold that thought." Ben reached for some more soap.

Grasping her hips, Cori pulled her back firmly. Ben looked over her shoulder and Cori captured her mouth in a kiss that was not at all gentle. She devoured her, alternately taking possession with her tongue and withdrawing to allow Ben to follow.

Ben moaned into Cori's mouth as she felt teeth close over her lower lip and when Cori sucked aggressively, Ben felt an answering tug low in her belly.

Cori rubbed her hands over the slick skin of Ben's stomach, slipping lower. When her fingers slid through wetness that had nothing to do with the water coursing over them, she thought she might lose the thin thread of control she still held. She forced herself to go slowly, only stroking broadly through the swollen folds when what she really wanted was to bury her fingers inside Ben's willing body.

Ben too was in danger of losing her mind. The solid feel of Cori pressed against the length of her back, the arms encircling her, and the fingers playing purposefully between her legs had her blood racing with need so strong it threatened to consume her. She rolled her hips back, pushing against Cori's thighs.

Ben's ass moving against her crotch spiked Cori's arousal. She sucked in a breath and fought the rising urge to take Ben savagely. She slid one hand up to cup Ben's breast. Her mouth closed over Ben's earlobe at the precise moment that her fingers reached Ben's nipple.

"Oh, God, Cori—please," Ben moaned, arching her back, seeking more contact. She could feel the effort of Cori's restraint. She understood Cori's need to be in control, yet she also understood the power she had in submitting. Somehow, she knew Cori would not take anything more than she was willing to give.

Cori raked her teeth down the side of Ben's neck, biting and sucking a path to her shoulder, where she closed them in earnest and marked Ben's skin.

"Cori, inside," Ben demanded, and when Cori complied, her knees threatened to buckle. She pressed her hands against the glass wall of the shower stall and braced herself to keep from sliding to the floor. As Cori thrust two and then three fingers inside Ben, she rocked her hips against Ben's backside.

"Let go," she urged, her mouth close to Ben's ear.

"So close," Ben ground out between clenched teeth. Her nearly shattering mind searched blindly for the words to tell Cori what would put her over the edge. "I need—"

She didn't get another word out before Cori's other hand pushed between her thighs and Ben felt the fingers she craved stroking firmly along her clit.

"Oh, that's it…" She squeezed her eyes shut and pressed her forehead against the glass as her body started to uncoil.

Ben's orgasm overtook her quickly. Her thrusting hips moved erratically and she shuddered with each stroke of Cori's fingers. Cori's name fell from her lips, melded with a string of unintelligible words.

Cori waited until Ben's body stopped pulsing around her fingers before she slowly withdrew them. Pressing one hand against the glass next to Ben's, she wrapped her free arm around Ben's waist.

"Cori?"

"Yes."

"I don't know if I can stand up much longer."

With a soft chuckle, Cori opened the shower door. Grabbing a large, fluffy towel, she wrapped it around Ben and kissed her.

"Thank you," Ben said, taking her hand and leading her toward the bedroom. "Now, come on. As soon as I regain my strength I have plans for you."

❖

Ben woke slowly, pleasantly aware of the warmth of Cori's body half covering her own. Her head rested on Ben's chest and one arm curled possessively around her ribs. A wonderful tightness in her stomach reminded Ben that several times during the night she had been coaxed into consciousness by Cori's lightly stroking fingers.

She sensed Cori's awakening in the almost imperceptible tensing of her muscles and the slight change in her breathing. As Cori surfaced, Ben remained still, wondering if Cori had any idea how cute and vulnerable she looked, rubbing her fist sleepily against her eyes.

"Good morning," she greeted softly when Cori turned her face upward. *Adorable.* Her sun-streaked hair stood up in spikes and her cobalt eyes were still hazy with sleep.

Cori tightened her arm around Ben, reluctant to move. Ben's skin was warm and her heart beat against Cori's cheek. She could get used to waking up like this. *Damn, what am I thinking?* She drew slowly away, shifting to pull the sheet more tightly around her.

"Do you want some coffee?" Ben sat up and slid toward the edge of the bed.

"I can't do this," Cori said quietly from behind her.

"What?" Ben turned.

"This isn't a good idea."

Ben reached for her and Cori slid out of her grasp. She didn't seem to think rationally when Ben was touching her. Instead she became a mass of emotion and sensation, losing herself in the possibilities that Ben's nearness promised. Her stomach churned as she stood and put some distance between herself and the woman still reclining in her bed.

This woman's talented hands and insistent mouth had completely shattered her the night before. She had, in the middle of the night, evoked a tenderness that Cori hadn't even known she was capable of. She had awakened once to find Ben curled against her side. Just lying there with her, warm and safe in the haven of their intimacy, affected Cori in ways she had never expected. All the times she had crawled away from some meaningless encounter were chased from her mind. True to the clichés, she had rarely stuck around for breakfast. This time, everything was different. Yet she needed to pretend it wasn't, so she could somehow do what she needed to do. *This can't happen. I can't allow it.*

"What are you talking about?" Ben demanded.

The panic and regret streaking across Cori's face nearly broke Ben's heart. *After all she said, was I just another in a long string of women? Could I really have been alone in what I felt...that there was something between us last night...something more than sex?*

Cori embarked on a line that was as familiar as breathing. It felt all wrong, but she had used it so often, the tone came automatically. "Look, last night was fun and all, but—"

"Fun?" Ben repeated in disbelief.

"Ben, be reasonable. We both know this can't go anywhere, so we should just quit while we're ahead." Cori slipped out of bed and pulled a T-shirt over her head.

"Actually, I didn't know it wasn't going anywhere," Ben said coolly. She stood and faced Cori across the bed. Her heart threatened to choke her.

"It's not like I made you any promises last night." Cori flung the words, her tone intentionally harsh. She *had* made a promise, in fact—to herself. And even if Ben couldn't see it now, she would be better off in the future, unburdened. Guilt flooded her as she watched hurt fill Ben's eyes. *Aw, hell.*

"Why are you angry with me?"

"I'm not angry! I'm—"

"What?" Ben demanded. Cori remained silent. "What, Cori? Just talk to me, damn it!"

I'm scared. "I really can't talk about it," Cori finally ground out, her voice rough with emotion.

Ben used all of her willpower to maintain the several feet that separated them. She wanted nothing more than to close the distance and take Cori in her arms, but they needed to have this conversation and it would not happen if she got close enough to touch her. She held tightly to the cold fist that had begun growing inside of her. She told herself that she should be angry—angry that Cori's regret threatened to tarnish the previous night.

"Don't do this," she said, realizing that Cori was working incredibly hard to push her away. *Why?*

"I have to," Cori said with terrible sadness.

"Why?" Ben tried to keep her panic in check. "Please, just tell me what's wrong and we can work it out together. I'm not afraid."

"But I am," Cori whispered. "You make me feel like I can do *anything.*"

With those words, Ben melted. "And that's bad?"

"There will come a day when I can't." Frustrated, Cori pushed her hand through her hair. "There are already days when I can't. And it's probably better if I just accept it now."

"Why? Why should you accept it? Cori, you *can* do anything. Certainly there will be times when things will be harder. But you have means and opportunities that a lot of people will never have—"

"Money doesn't solve *this*," Cori said, but Ben rushed on.

"I'm not saying that it does. I *am* saying that life is what you make of it. And this disease—anything in life, really—can only define you if you allow it to." Now Ben did move toward her, desperate to stop what she feared what was about to happen. The wall Cori was erecting between them was practically tangible. "Cori. I…care about you."

As Ben moved, Cori jerked back. She was so intent on staying out of Ben's reach that she staggered back two steps and promptly fell over the chair by the door. Ben leapt forward to help her up, but Cori was already stumbling to her feet.

"Ben, I'm sorry. I didn't mean to hurt you, but I just can't…" Cori's voice trailed off as her eyes met Ben's and found tears welling there. *Oh, God, don't look at me like that.* She couldn't find the words. "I—I'm sorry," she whispered and fled to the bathroom, closing and locking the door behind her.

Cori leaned against the inside of the door. For several long minutes she heard shuffling noises that she soon placed as the rustling of clothing being hastily pulled on. She expected anger, she was used to anger. After all, this wasn't the first time she'd had to let down a woman who expected more than just one night. It was the first time that it tore her apart. Remnants of their night together lingered on Cori's skin. But she kept seeing the misery in Ben's eyes as she tried to convince her to trust, and a sharp stab of pain accompanied the soft click of the bedroom door closing. She slid down to sit on the floor and wrapped her arms around her knees in an attempt to ease the ache in her stomach.

CHAPTER SIXTEEN

The morning sun burned brightly, showing no mercy for Cori's aching eyes. She scowled and pulled her sunglasses from her head and slipped them on. It did not seem quite fair that the sky should be so blue and the temperature a perfect seventy-three degrees. Nor did she appreciate the gentle breeze that ruffled her hair as she sat at one of the quaint little wrought-iron tables outside a coffee shop with a view of the park. She grumbled to herself and absently stirred the cappuccino that tasted entirely too decadent for her mood.

"Hungover again?" Gretchen approached, carrying her usual cup of black coffee and a blueberry muffin.

"Bite me," Cori growled.

"That's pleasant." Sitting opposite Cori, she pulled a folded magazine from under her arm and slapped it down on the table.

Cori glanced at it, recognizing the cover of *Canvassed*. She forced herself to look away casually.

"Do you want to tell me what's going on or should I guess?" Gretchen asked dryly. Cori didn't respond. "I read the article, so I know something is up."

"There's nothing out of sorts in that article." Cori had read it too. Once again she had found Ben's work to be fair and respectful, while also being honest and easy to read. She had scoured the page for a hint that Ben was at least one fraction as miserable as she was and had found nothing.

"Sure, not in the article alone," Gretchen conceded. "I'm talking about you walking around like someone stole your puppy."

"I am not."

"And the way you bristle like a porcupine every time someone even mentions Ben's name."

"Oh, fuck off," Cori exclaimed in exasperation.

"See."

It was futile to argue. No matter what she said, Gretchen would turn it around on her.

"Spill," Gretchen demanded, setting down her muffin and giving Cori her most intimidating stare.

"I slept with her," Cori blurted out.

"You what?"

"You heard me."

"When?"

"A couple of weeks ago, on our last day together."

"Okay," Gretchen drew the word out as she considered Cori's words. "So what's the problem? She's certainly not the first. I mean, it's not like you spent the night…" Gretchen trailed off at Cori's guilty expression. "*You spent the night?*"

Cori pushed her fingers through her hair. "I don't know what the hell I was thinking."

"Are you going to see her again?"

"No." She broke a piece off Gretchen's muffin and popped it into her mouth.

"Do you want to?" Gretchen asked cautiously.

Cori paused. She didn't have to think about her answer, but that was part of the problem. She had no doubt. She wanted to, again and again. Unfortunately her life was no longer just about what *she* wanted.

"Oh, boy." Gretchen heard the answer in Cori's silence.

"Yeah," Cori breathed.

"What are you going to do?"

"Nothing." Cori feigned indifference, sipping her cappuccino.

"Nothing?"

"There's nothing I can do, Gretchen. It's not an option."

"But—"

"It's not open for discussion."

"I could talk to her. She's a real person. She'll understand."

"It's too late for that," Cori said. "Trust me. I hurt her."

❖

Ben breezed through the crowded baggage claim area of McCarran International Airport. She had packed light for the two-day trip, fitting everything into a carry-on so she wouldn't have to wait for her bags. She stepped outside and was immediately assailed by the hot, dry Nevada air. She suddenly remembered why she hated the desert, but she forged on, climbing into the back of a waiting cab and directing the driver to take her to the Mirage. He flipped the meter on and headed for the strip.

Less than an hour later, having checked in and dropped her bag at her room, Ben was on her way back down to the main level. She had glanced at the map in her room, and when she exited the elevator, she made her way through the casino, following the various signs to the Danny Gans Theatre. But she got turned around and ended up asking a bellman for directions.

She wondered for perhaps the tenth time if it had been such a good idea to take this assignment. She had been failing miserably at distracting herself from thoughts of Cori. After leaving the apartment that night, she had gone home and shut herself away for the next few days, only dragging herself out of bed to write the articles Mitchell was hounding her for. They would be in three separate monthly issues, and only the first was due right away. However, she did them all at once, quickly, like ripping off a Band-aid. It was excruciating.

When she was done she rewarded herself with one more evening spent moping in bed. The next morning she decided she would not allow her foolish feelings for Cori Saxton to rule her life. It wasn't as though she had ever expected Cori to care; they were completely unalike and she had known that from day one. It certainly wasn't the end of the world.

When the offer to interview Robin Sparks came along, Ben decided it must be a sign. The rising young comedienne was doing a series of shows in Las Vegas, and the fact that the job would take her practically to the other side of the country, even for just a couple of days, made it even more appealing.

Ben followed the directions given to her by the woman at the box office, weaving a convoluted path through the backstage area. As she approached her destination, a lime green dressing-room door, Ben ran through in her mind the facts she already knew about her subject. Robin Sparks had gotten her start in San Antonio after winning a local talent contest. She had spent the ensuing three years touring the country with two other comics. She did live stand-up but was also making occasional appearances on the Comedy Channel.

Ben's knock was answered by a voice telling her to enter. She opened the door to find a tiny room barely large enough to accommodate two chairs and a clothing rack. Robin occupied the one in front of the mirror, patiently having her make-up applied.

They exchanged introductions as Ben settled into the other chair. She held up a tape recorder in silent question and Robin nodded.

"You've been touring for a few years now, haven't you?" Ben asked after clicking on the recorder.

"Paying my dues," Robin said. "College bars, seedy comedy clubs, a few reputable ones, we went wherever we could make a buck. But, hey, I can't complain, can I? It got me here. Vegas is the big time, you know what I mean?"

Ben nodded, enjoying Robin's Texas drawl. Barely twenty-three years old, Robin didn't look a day over legal. So when Ben found her attention drawn to long legs enticingly displayed in the shortest of skirts, she jerked back up. A slow grin spread across Robin's face and Ben realized she'd been caught.

"A little trick I learned in Texas. Good ol' boys, you know. Just show enough leg and they'll applaud all night. Get a few ladies who appreciate it too," she finished with a wink.

Oh hell, straight girls are trouble. Ben forced her thoughts back to the interview. She managed to get through the rest of her questions without incident. They finished up only minutes before Robin was due to go on.

"You should stick around after the show. We'll have a drink,"

Robin suggested as she headed for the stage. She didn't wait for Ben's response, seeming to take for granted that the answer would be yes.

"She don't mean just a drink."

Ben turned at the voice from behind her. The make-up artist she hadn't bothered to notice was standing there.

"What do you mean?"

"I usually don't say anything, but—you seemed real nice during your interview and all. And I just didn't want my sister to treat you like all the others."

This is Robin's sister? They couldn't be more different. Robin's hair had the varying shades of a field of wheat and fell in loose curls to brush her shoulders. This woman's long, black hair was cut in a simple, straight style and tucked behind her ears. Ben would bet a month's salary that the aqua color of Robin's eyes was the result of contact lenses, unlike her sister's dark eyes, which looked back at Ben from behind wire-rimmed glasses that she pushed nervously up her nose with one finger.

"It's very nice to meet you—uh—"

"Patti."

"Patti, I'm sorry, Robin didn't tell me you two were related." Ben realized that as they had talked, Robin hadn't bothered to introduce her make-up artist at all. "How long have you been working for Robin?"

"I don't. Not really. I mean, she don't actually pay me," Patti explained.

Ben glanced at her watch. "Well, Patti, it was nice to meet you. I'm going to go out front and catch some of Robin's show before I take off." She started for the door that led to the audience. "Oh, and I have no intention of taking your sister up on her offer," she added as an afterthought.

Patti smiled before turning back to packing up her cosmetics.

After the show, Ben headed back to her room, all too aware that the next day she would return to New York and be faced with finding another distraction. She settled on the bed with her laptop, transferring her notes. A king-sized bed. If she had thought her bed at home felt lonely, this one felt positively solitary. She forced her attention to the notes in front of her. As she read over them she realized it wouldn't take her long at all to write this article.

Ironically, Robin actually *was* as one-dimensional as Ben had once thought Cori would be.

❖

Cori sat alone at the end of her dock swinging her feet gently. For the fourth night in a row she stared at the setting sun, trying to summon the energy to return to the house and cook another solitary dinner. As the last sliver of nearly crimson light slipped below the horizon, Cori stood.

She wandered restlessly through the house, frustrated with her inability to relax in what was supposed to be her safe haven. *Damn it, this is why I never brought women here. Now this place is tainted.* After only a couple of days, Ben's memory was all over the house. It wasn't just the house, she admitted. Ben was everywhere she looked these days. She kept waiting for it to get better. Surely eventually she would begin to forget how it felt to hold Ben, to kiss her or just to sit with her curled up at opposite ends of the sofa. At least, that had been the plan when she had once again fled upstate early that week. She had been prowling her house ever since to no avail.

When she walked back out onto the deck, fighting off a vision of Ben leaning against the railing holding a glass of wine, Cori thought absurdly that she was probably going to have to sell the place. *Sure, sell it. Start fresh someplace else.* She'd passed a cute little cabin farther downriver on the drive up. *What the hell am I thinking? I'm not selling my house over some woman.* But the fact that Ben was not just any woman was becoming far too evident as the days passed.

Shoving her hands into her hair, she headed for the only part of the house that she had yet to pace in. As she descended the stairs to her studio, an idea started forming in her mind. She needed to exorcise some demons, and damn it, it had been long enough. She barely paused at the bottom of the staircase before she plunged into the room.

Crossing to the center of the studio, she set about preparing her workspace. She put a fresh canvas on an easel and set up a palette of the colors needed to create the vision swimming behind her eyes.

Taking a deep breath, Cori closed her eyes and freely allowed the image to drift into her mind. She could sometimes see a completed painting in her head even before she touched brush to canvas. As the colors coalesced behind her eyelids, Cori had a brief glimpse of what she wanted to capture, and it imprinted in her mind before she opened her eyes once more.

Pushing her brush into several paints, she expertly mixed the hue she needed. She glanced only for a second at the pure, blank expanse before lifting her hand and swiping her brush against the canvas.

Cori worked feverishly for several hours, desperate to capture as much as she could as quickly as possible. The night faded into the wee hours of the morning, but she barely noticed. As she worked, another idea germinated. It lingered in the back of her mind. When she finally set her brush down, she stepped back and considered her progress, tilting her head from side to side. Now that her mind was not as occupied with painting, her new plan pushed its way forward insistently. She spent the next hour working out the details in her head as she touched up the painting.

Inhaling the familiar smell of paint and linseed oil, she finally studied her work. Warm pleasure hummed beneath the relief that flooded her. She had captured exactly the image in her mind. Whatever else happened, she would have this canvas and would remember the flash of moments that had inspired it. Motivated by both the painting and the ideas that had been building while she worked, Cori dug her cell phone out of her pocket and flipped it open.

"I painted," she said as soon as Gretchen picked up.

"What?"

"I painted," Cori repeated. "Last night. And it felt good. So, I was thinking. I need to have a show sometime soon."

"I have a list of gallery owners who have been waiting for the call." Gretchen paused. An uncertain note entered her voice. "It's early days. Are you sure you'll be able to sustain this?"

"Yes. Everything has changed. I can work again."

"That's wonderful. I was worried after the articles when you ran away upstate again."

"Well, I'm back now. Oh, and Gretchen…not a gallery. Something bigger. And there's more." Cori explained her plans for a joint show with several of her peers. It would really be a fund-raiser of sorts.

"We'll need some press, television probably. But Mitch will probably want Ben—"

"No," Cori interrupted.

"Why?"

"Don't call Mitch. In fact, I don't want any press releases. This is by invitation only." She'd already decided that the show would be exclusive, and any necessary press releases could be made afterward. The selective guest list she was putting together would fuel talk among all the right people, anyway.

"Cori, something like this needs media coverage. Whatever is going on between you and Ben—"

"There's nothing going on between me and Ben," Cori said and then acquiesced on one point. "I'll put some of the media on the guest list, but I'll pick which ones."

CHAPTER SEVENTEEN

W hy is your mailman downstairs cursing you?" Lucy asked as Ben opened the door. Without waiting for a reply, she headed for the kitchen to deposit the grocery bags she carried.

"Shit. I haven't checked my mail all week. Be right back." Ben rushed out.

When she returned, Lucy was in the kitchen unpacking ice cream, hot fudge, and cookies. Ben glanced at the spread and then at her cousin with a raised eyebrow.

"What? It's movie night, I'm allowed." Lucy had declared it a girls' night in. They planned to spend the evening lounging in Ben's apartment in sweats, watching movies.

Ben shrugged and set about sorting through the stack of envelopes she'd had to pry out of her small mailbox. Junk mail went directly into the trash and bills in a stack to be opened later. She was left with a small square envelope in her hand. She slid the thick card out and read the words twice before they sank in.

"So which movie do you want to watch first?" Lucy asked, turning away from the freezer. "What is it?"

She saw the blank look on Ben's face and the card still loosely clasped in Ben's hand. Numbly, Ben handed it over.

"You and a guest are cordially invited…" Lucy's voice trailed off as she finished reading to herself. She looked up at Ben. "This is an invitation to a reception and art show for the Saxton Foundation."

Ben nodded.

"What's the Saxton Foundation?"

"Never heard of it." Ben's indifference was forced. "Let's watch the comedy first."

"Ben, this thing is tonight. When was the last time you checked your mail?"

Ben had to think about that one. "Last week. I think."

"Okay. Come on." Lucy pulled Ben toward the bedroom.

"What are you doing?" Ben resisted, but Lucy continued to yank on her arm.

"We still have time. You're getting dressed and going down there."

"There's no point."

Ben dug in her feet. Lucy stopped and stared at her.

"You've been moping over her for weeks."

"Yeah, but she turned me away. Or have you forgotten that?"

Lucy moved behind her and started pushing her forward. "Then why did she send you this invitation? You have to go and see what this is about. Now get in there and put on your sexiest little black dress."

Ben relented, reluctant to admit that she too was curious about what had prompted the invitation. "Okay, but you're going with me."

"I'll go home and get dressed and pick you up in an hour."

❖

The next time Ben opened her door to Lucy they were both a good deal more presentable. Lucy had left her hair down. Her dark green dress hugged her curves as if it were made for her. Lucy stepped inside and circled Ben with a low whistle.

"Nice," she murmured.

Ben smiled. She'd considered a cocktail dress but, on a whim, had put on the gray pinstripe suit over a rose-colored silk shell. She worried that the suit was not formal enough for the affair, but after checking her reflection in the mirror she changed her mind. Cori had exquisite taste. And though bought off the rack, the suit was cut perfectly for her. Ben added a simple pair of large gold hoop earrings and left her neckline bare. She was glad she'd opted for an easy up-do; the simple hairstyle drew attention to her high cheekbones and slender neck.

"It's perfect," Lucy said. "She'll wonder what the hell she was thinking."

"Let's hope so." Ben began to allow a sliver of hope. By now, maybe Cori regretted pushing her away.

"I have a cab waiting downstairs," Lucy said, following Ben out and waiting while she locked up.

Several blocks later they climbed out of the cab and walked into the spacious lobby of the Carlyle Hotel.

"Damn," Lucy hissed.

If Ben needed a reminder that they were grossly outclassed by Cori's circle, her cousin's awestruck expression would do the trick. Ben tried not to gape at the highly polished floor, chandelier, and impressive molding. Several couples walked past them, their confident gaits screamed entitlement.

"Listen, you may be getting used to these highbrow parties, but this is all new to me," Lucy said.

"Please, behave," Ben urged as they fell in with a group of people making their way toward the reception room reserved for the Saxton Foundation.

"I can't make any promises." Lucy stopped short as she and Ben stepped through the wide doorway. Her eyes locked on a figure across the room. "Good Lord, the woman is positively edible."

Ben followed her gaze and drew a sharp breath. Cori stood among a small group of people. Ben had the impression of several blurry faces, but all she could see was Cori, both elegant and powerful in a black tuxedo-cut suit. Instead of the traditional white shirt, she wore an ash gray one left open at the collar. Her hair looked like someone had had their hands buried in it only minutes before. Ben suspected this was deliberate. Her palms itched and she was overwhelmed with the urge to push her own hands through the fair tresses, staking a claim. *She looks good. Who am I kidding? Lucy is right, positively edible.* Unbidden, Ben's mind filled with the memory of running her tongue over Cori's skin.

"Are you going to go talk to her?"

"No," Ben answered quickly.

"Um, then what are we doing here?"

"Oh, God. I don't know."

"Okay, just calm down." Lucy drew her farther into the room, grabbed two glasses of champagne from a passing waiter, and pressed one into Ben's hand.

At the ringing of silverware against crystal they turned. Cori tapped a fork against her glass and stepped up to a podium at the far end of the room.

"Ladies and gentlemen, I'd like to thank you all for joining me here tonight." Cori scanned the room, making eye contact with many familiar faces. "We are here to announce the formation of the Saxton Foundation." Her voice nearly faltered as her eyes came to rest on Ben's face. Then she sought Gretchen's, casting an accusatory look before returning to Ben. She swallowed the lump forming in the back of her throat and forced herself to go on. "A wise person once reminded me that I am fortunate enough to have means and opportunity that many will never have. Growing up, I was lucky enough to go to a well-funded private school where my artistic pursuits were nurtured and given the chance to flourish. When I began thinking about what I might be able to give back to the community, it was only natural that I look to the arts."

She explained that the Saxton Foundation would contribute to the art programs of local public schools in an effort to enhance the opportunities for less privileged students. It would also establish several scholarships to be granted each year to deserving students wishing to further their education in the arts.

"So, in closing, with a few exceptions, the paintings you see displayed here tonight are available for purchase. All proceeds will, of course, go to the foundation. In addition to myself, several other area artists have generously donated their work to this show. Please, enjoy yourselves."

Amidst a polite smattering of applause, Lucy leaned close to Ben and whispered, "She looked right at you."

"I know."

❖

Cori wandered smoothly through the crowd, accepting congratulations. Occasionally, she paused long enough to grasp a hand and engage in polite conversation. She sipped from a flute of champagne and nodded her head appropriately until such time as she sensed an opening in the conversation. Apologetically mumbling something about her duties as hostess, she shrugged her shoulders in a way she knew would be seen as charming and moved on to the next person. She worked her way across the room in this manner, effortlessly, the ever-attentive hostess. *Mother would be proud,* she thought cynically. After all, this *was* what Saxton women were born and bred to do.

Gretchen caught up with her just as she had finally managed to tuck herself into a shadowy corner of the room. Cori leaned casually against the wall, her relaxed posture belying her nervousness.

"What's wrong?"

Hearing the edge in Gretchen's voice, Cori remained silent.

Gretchen moved closer and lowered her voice. "I know you, Cori. What's going on?"

"Is everyone enjoying the show?" Cori ignored Gretchen's question.

"Are you asking about anyone in particular?"

"Leave it alone, Gretchen." Cori tossed back her champagne in one gulp. "Please." she asked, softly, letting her eyes travel to the one person she needed to see but knew she should avoid.

Gretchen followed Cori's gaze. Ben was carefully making her way around the outside edge of the room, pausing in front of each painting. A striking redhead at her side grabbed her arm and leaned close.

"I wasn't sure if she would come." Gretchen watched Cori's eyes narrow as she took in the familiar way the redhead touched Ben.

"So you *did* do this," Cori accused, her suspicions confirmed.

"I just sent her an invitation. What happens next is up to the two of you."

Cori's eyes tracked Ben as she moved from canvas to canvas. Her heart pounded hard in her chest as each step brought her unknowingly closer to the canvas that would unveil Cori's emotions.

The fact that Ben would first see it with another woman on her arm tore at Cori's heart. Apparently, some things had changed in the weeks since they'd seen each other.

❖

"She really is very talented," Lucy commented as they stood before the darkly intense painting Ben had seen on the easel in Cori's studio. "What? She is," Lucy said when Ben only glared at her. "This one is so different, though."

"That's what I said when I first saw it." Ben hadn't understood why at the time, but now, something inside of her twisted as she lost herself in the painting. *Oh, Cori, what you must have been going through.* It was a powerful piece in its own right. But it was made more so when viewed with a full understanding of the artist. Emotion washed over her as she stared at the melding colors— alternately fiery and cold at the same time. She ached for Cori, for the uncertainty in her future, and that Cori felt she must sentence herself to facing it all alone.

Lucy's sharp gasp drew Ben's attention. She stood several feet away, wide-eyed in front of another painting.

Ben's breath caught in her throat as she moved to Lucy's side to see what was so earth-shattering. Her own larger-than-life image stared back at her. *This is how she sees me?* Cori had painted her with a radiant smile that lit her expression as if from the inside. She had perfectly captured the amber shade of her eyes and the slight wrinkle at their corners when she smiled. Ben's tousled hair fell in soft waves to frame her high cheekbones and the sleek line of her jaw. She'd never imagined that anyone could look at her and see such beauty. Seeing herself through Cori's eyes shook her.

"Jesus, Ben, you're beautiful," Lucy whispered reverently, still staring at the painting.

"Yes, she is." Cori's slight rasp scraped against her raw emotions.

Ben stiffened. She'd come to the show because she couldn't have stayed away. But she knew now that she hadn't really been prepared—already, being this close was rending the place in her soul that existed only for Cori, and she hadn't even turned to face her yet.

She finally did, her stomach clenching involuntarily when a familiar spicy scent teased her consciousness. With some effort, Ben was able to bring her reaction under control, and when her eyes met Cori's resolutely, she knew they were devoid of emotion.

"It seems that you do portraits quite well after all," Ben remarked flatly.

"Actually I think this was a—um, special project." Cori struggled to keep her voice even. "And I was right about the suit. It looks great on you." Her heart twisted at the distance she saw in Ben's eyes, but she worked to keep her feelings hidden She had watched from the corner of the room, her insides coiling tightly in anticipation, while Ben approached the painting. Unable to resist, she crossed the room because she wanted to see Ben's reaction to this piece. She searched Ben's face, looking for any sign that the painting had touched something in her. What she found was a carefully guarded expression.

Her attention shifted to the redhead at Ben's side, and she was suddenly filled with doubt. There wasn't a day that had gone by since they met that Cori hadn't thought about Ben. From very early on, the connection she felt to her ran deeper than with any woman before. And despite everything that had happened between them, she had thought the feeling was mutual. However, it seemed Ben had moved on.

The woman who stood so comfortably next to her was attractive. Her copper curls fell to her shoulders, just barely touching the pale skin left bare there. She was fashionably clad in a green silk dress that perfectly matched her sparkling eyes. Eyes that now regarded Cori warily.

Ben watched the two women size each other up. She would have expected Lucy's protective glare; however, her heart lifted when she saw the blatant jealousy in Cori's expression. Grasping Lucy's arm just above her elbow, Ben pulled her closer. Cori's eyes darkened considerably.

"Cori Saxton, this is Lucy Andrews." She waited a beat before adding, "My cousin."

"It's nice to meet you." Cori couldn't hide her rush of relief.

"I've heard a lot about you," Lucy said.

Taking advantage of Cori's diverted attention while she exchanged pleasantries with Lucy, Ben feasted her eyes. It seemed like forever since she had seen Cori, but her image was indelible. Ben hadn't realized it was possible to feel so incomplete without another person. Or that totality could come simply from being near Cori. But it did. A place that had been hollow was suddenly filled as she was unable to pull her eyes from the face of the woman she loved. *I love her?*

Struggling with a mini–panic attack over that thought, she was vaguely aware of Lucy complimenting Cori.

"I think it's great what you're doing with this charity. And the work you're displaying here today is amazing." She gestured toward the portrait of Ben. "It's exceptional."

"Thanks. I was—inspired." Cori was losing the fight to avoid looking at Ben. The compulsion was too much and she surrendered to it with a fatalistic sigh. It was too late to pretend she could control herself completely around this woman.

"Ah—well, I guess." Lucy seemed to be searching for a polite way to excuse herself. "Yeah," she said, finally giving up on tact and slipping away.

Neither Ben nor Cori noticed her departure.

"It—it really is an amazing painting. You made me look so much—better," Ben said after several long moments.

"You're gorgeous." Cori gazed at Ben standing there beside her portrait, and she thought she had failed. *You are so much more than I could ever capture in mere paint.* "It's so good to see you. I've missed your face." It was an odd thing to say considering she had spent countless hours envisioning Ben's face as she worked on the portrait. But it made perfect sense to her.

"I've missed you too," Ben whispered.

"I've got to hang around here for a while, but—will you stay? Can we get a cup of coffee or something afterward?"

There was something endearing about the tentativeness of Cori's invitation. "Yes. I'll wait."

Ben kept her word, watching Cori from across the room as

she moved among the crowd talking to guests. Lucy returned with champagne, and Ben tried unsuccessfully to draw her attention from Cori, who also cast periodic glances her way. But after a while there seemed no point in fighting it.

"So, what's going on?" Lucy asked.

"She wants to talk after the party."

"Is that good?"

"I think so." Ben forced her gaze back to Lucy. "She didn't really say, but there was something…"

"Ben, it's nice to see you again." Gretchen approached them. She clasped Ben's hand tightly. "I'm *so* glad you could make it." Her tone of voice conveyed more than a polite greeting. "And I know Cori must be very happy to see you."

Ben smiled and introduced Lucy.

"Cori's work is amazing, especially that one of Ben," Lucy gushed.

"I know. It was right after I saw it for the first time that I sent your invitation."

"I didn't pose for it." Ben was not quite sure why she said that. She was trying to explain the painting to herself, and nothing she came up with made any sense.

Gretchen seemed to understand her confusion. "She just told me one day that she had started painting again. And then she spilled all of her plans about starting the foundation and what she hoped it would accomplish in the future. But as soon as I saw this painting I figured you must have had something to do with the change in her."

"I—no, I haven't even seen her in weeks," Ben protested.

"Well, maybe not directly, then."

Ben stared at the painting, trying to make sense of Gretchen's words. *It really is an incredible likeness, so detailed.* Surely the fact that Cori put the time and effort into this meant something. Ben's heart flooded with optimism. Maybe there was a chance.

"What an amazing piece."

Ben cringed at the sound of a voice behind her. She had only heard it once before but she would never forget it. She caught a look of apprehension on Gretchen's face and turned to find Veronica studying the painting next to Ben's portrait, the one that Cori had kept on her easel as a reminder every day while she couldn't work.

"Oh, hello." Veronica noticed them standing there. She pointedly ignored Ben and addressed Gretchen. "I'll take it."

"It's not for sale," Cori said from behind Ben. She stepped into their circle. Veronica immediately crossed to her.

Ben tensed and felt Lucy's hand on her arm.

"Why, Cori, I think we could work out some kind of arrangement, don't you?" Veronica purred, sliding closer.

Ben fought the urge to step between them and claw the woman's eyes out. She didn't consider herself a violent person, but she had never felt such strong dislike for someone in her life. It was only Lucy's restraining hand that kept her from leaping across the space that separated them.

Cori purposefully uncurled Veronica's fingers from around her arm and moved out of reach. "It's not for sale."

"Well, why not? It's just a painting." Veronica's tone of voice indicated that she clearly thought that everything had its price.

"Actually, it's more than just a painting," Cori corrected her. "It's a reminder." She looked at Ben for several long seconds and then glanced at the portrait behind her. "They both are. Now if you'll excuse me, the guests are starting to leave and I really must thank them for attending."

As she passed, she touched the small of Ben's back so fleetingly that if it weren't for the tingling sensation left behind Ben might have thought she imagined it.

Casting a look of disbelief at Cori's retreating back, Veronica stalked away.

"Who invited her?" Lucy grumbled, obviously having figured out who Veronica was.

"No one," Gretchen said sharply. "She must have managed to talk someone into bringing her as their guest, because she sure wasn't on the list."

CHAPTER EIGHTEEN

S o they really aren't for sale." Ben stood shoulder to shoulder with Cori, both of them staring at the paintings. True to her word, Ben had waited until the room cleared, and now they were the only remaining occupants.

She had been elated when Cori refused to sell the painting to Veronica, but she hadn't thought Cori would seriously hold on to them. Especially when a silver-haired dapperly dressed gentleman had murmured a figure that had nearly caused Ben to choke on a mouthful of champagne. Without blinking, Cori had politely declined. The man saluted her resolve and then generously offered the same sum for a different painting. All of the others had eventually been sold at a great profit for the Saxton Foundation.

"No. They're not."

"It was an amazing night, Cori. You should be proud of yourself."

"I should?" Cori didn't look at her.

"Yes. You figured out how to use your gifts to do something that will matter to a lot of kids. Who knows how many will have a future they might not have had if it weren't for you." Ben made a conscious effort to keep her voice even despite her racing heart.

"I'm glad you came, Ben."

"You are?"

Cori was quiet for a moment. There were so many things to say and so many she wondered if she would ever be able to say. "Would you like to go get some coffee? Or, well, don't take this the wrong way, but my place is just a couple of blocks away." She rushed on nervously before Ben could respond. "It's just that I'd like to be able to talk to you privately. It seems like I haven't gotten more than a moment with you all night, and—"

Without thinking, Ben pressed two fingers to Cori's lips to silence her. There was that damn tingling sensation again. She jerked her hand back. "Your place is fine."

❖

Ben followed Cori inside her apartment and laid her purse on the hall table. She longed to blurt out her feelings. Remaining silent during the walk from the hotel had been excruciating, but Cori seemed disinclined to speak, so Ben had not pressed the point.

"Can I get you something to drink?" Cori asked.

"No, thank you." Ben perched on the edge of the sofa.

Cori remained standing. She slipped out of her jacket and draped it over the back of a nearby chair. Ben watched as she took off her cuff links and tucked them in the pocket of her jacket. She shook her sleeves loose and pushed them up her forearms. For a moment, Ben allowed herself to imagine how nice it would be to come home with Cori after an evening out and undress her. They would plop down on the sofa next to each other, prop their feet up on the coffee table, and talk about who wore what to the party.

"Ben, this isn't going to work." Cori was pacing a few feet away.

"Yeah. You said that before. So you brought me back here to tell me that again?" Ben felt her moment slipping away, but there remained a glimmer of hope when she recalled the way Cori had looked at her less than an hour earlier.

She moved to stand in front of Cori, stopping her progress. Ben realized she felt not a second's hesitation about Cori's uncertain future, only an overwhelming need to touch her. Setting caution aside, she pulled Cori into her arms. She could feel Cori's heart beating against her own as their chests pressed closely together.

"Don't you understand? My life has changed irrevocably." Cori tried to pull back but Ben held on.

"Yes, I know, darling. Mine did too—the day I got out of Henry's truck and saw you standing there on your porch." Ben cupped Cori's jaw, realizing the truth of her words. She couldn't have known it at the time, but she hadn't been the same since she'd squinted up at Cori's silhouetted figure.

"Damn it, Ben!" Cori jerked out of her embrace. She needed the distance between them to keep her resolve intact. "You're being purposely obtuse. I'm trying to tell you that I'm not going to get better. There's no cure. I'll only get progressively worse."

"I know, you've said that too," Ben said quietly.

"The only thing that remains to be seen is how much worse and how fast." Saying the words aloud brought a flood of panic into Cori's heart, but she needed Ben to understand what was at stake. She needed Ben to walk away now, because if she didn't, Cori would give in to the crazy urge to submit to her.

"I know." Ben's voice remained steady. "I know all of that."

"I have nothing to give you. What if I can't paint? I'm nothing without my work."

The anguish in Cori's voice was so palpable that it made Ben's chest ache, and she was unsure if she would ever be able to convince Cori to look beyond her fears—to see the heart Ben was offering now in her outstretched hands.

"Sweetheart, you can't believe that. You proved tonight that you have something else to offer. You are an amazing artist. But your art is simply a reflection of your soul, not a testament of your worth. You have more value than just the price tag on your paintings."

Cori shook her head as if she could deny Ben's words. "A year ago I would have jumped at the chance to be involved with a smart, sexy—"

"No, you wouldn't have," Ben interrupted.

"I wouldn't have?"

"No, you were still dating bimbos," Ben explained bluntly. "You wouldn't have looked twice at me."

"Yes, I would have," Cori argued, though she knew Ben was probably right.

"No. You needed the events of the past year to let you know what is important. You needed to take a good look at what you want from life."

"Ben…" Cori's intention was to stop her before she no longer had any defenses against the words.

Ben moved to close the distance between them, feeling as if her whole future depended upon that moment, on her ability to make Cori see what was in her soul. She laid her hand gently against the middle of Cori's chest and drew strength from the steady beat beneath her palm. "So, Cori Saxton, what is it that you want from life?"

"Ben, I can't." Cori couldn't bear to see the naked emotion in Ben's eyes. She could feel the warmth of Ben's hand through the thin layer of her shirt. Her mind screamed to step away, but she couldn't make herself move. Her body was acting on its own and was reluctant to lose that tiny physical connection between them.

Ben took a deep breath. "I need you to tell me. What do you want? Because I want *you*, whatever time brings, I want to be there beside you—to face it with you." She had done it. She had stepped off the edge of a cliff, and there was no going back.

"It could hurt," Cori said cautiously.

"Yes. And when it does, we'll hold each other."

"And when I can't hold you?"

"*If* you can't hold me, then I will hold you."

"Ben, it's really not that simple. Someday—"

"It is that simple. You're strong now. I'll deal with someday when it happens."

"You can't just push reality aside and say you'll deal with it later."

"I also can't ignore the way I feel about you now because I'm afraid of what the future may bring. I want *you*, Cori. Whatever that entails, I'll take it. I'll risk the future in exchange for the way you make me feel right now."

She was running out of excuses, and Ben's hand still resting against her chest was making it more and more difficult to think. "How do I make you feel?" She was stalling.

"I asked you first. What do you want?"

Cori covered Ben's hand, pressing it more tightly against her chest. *You're so good for me.*

"You don't let me get away with anything. I've never had that. Even before—" She choked on the words. "Before I got sick. All of my life people have catered to me because of who I am or who my parents are. You don't do that. In fact, I've sometimes wondered if you're impressed by anything at all about me. But when you speak, when you look at me, I never have to wonder if you're sincere. I want you, of course. Do you really not know that?" Cori drew her close and kissed her tenderly, fearing she could break the tenuous thread that was forming between them.

Ben pressed her face into Cori's neck and wrapped her arms tightly around her waist. "You make *me* feel as if I can do anything," she said, borrowing Cori's words. "And I've never had that before."

"Ben, I don't know how to do this." Cori's fingers danced faintly along her spine. "Hell, I've never really done the relationship thing."

Ben laughed softly. "I'll try to be gentle." She kissed up the side of Cori's neck and drew her earlobe into her mouth.

"If you keep that up…" Cori gasped at the scrape of Ben's teeth.

"What are you going to do about it?" Ben pulled the back of Cori's shirt free and slid her hands over warm skin as soft as silk.

"I'll show you," Cori replied, backing her into the bedroom.

"Hmm…" Ben pressed a hand to the center of Cori's chest, stopping her. She continued backward, putting some space between them. A teasing light sparked in her eyes. "I don't know. Are you well? I mean, I wouldn't want to tax your system."

Cori raised an eyebrow. "Not well?" Ben remained silent but a smile tugged at the corners of her mouth. "Tax my system, eh?" Cori advanced on her. "Maybe I need to show you just how capable I am."

Ben's stomach tightened pleasantly as a feral grin intensified Cori's gaze. "How exactly do you plan to do that?" she teased.

Cori stopped before her, mere inches between them. "Take this off," she demanded, tugging at Ben's lapel.

Ben complied without question, stripping off both the jacket and the silk beneath. Cori's confidence was sexy as hell, and Ben had no problem letting her take control.

"This too." Cori brushed her fingers lightly over the lacy cup of Ben's bra. She reveled in the reaction of Ben's flesh through the fabric.

After dropping her bra to the floor, Ben reached automatically for the waistband of her slacks, but Cori stopped her.

"Not yet." Power surged through Cori and she struggled to control her fervor. She had never felt stronger than she did standing there gazing at Ben. Her arousal climbed rapidly and she was once again overwhelmed with the desire to take Ben quickly and passionately. Yet a bigger part of her needed to exercise control—over herself as much as over Ben. Her desire for restraint came not from a need to prove something, but from the desire to bring Ben as much pleasure as she could. She silently acknowledged the fact that she had selfish intentions as well. She wanted to memorize every moment she spent touching Ben.

Ben obediently dropped her hands to her side. Cori slowly lifted her hand and brushed her fingers feather-light over one nipple, Ben's breath hissing through her teeth as her nipple tightened. Cori drew two fingers down the center of Ben's chest, between her breasts and moving lower. The sensitive skin of her abdomen jumped as Cori's fingers trailed over it.

Ben fought to stand still, but her body strained toward Cori's fingers, seeking to increase their pressure. She didn't quite manage to stifle a moan, but she did bite back the plea that rose up in her throat.

Heart racing, Cori attempted to draw a calming breath. She traced her hand back up to cup Ben's jaw firmly, her thumb under Ben's jawbone and her fingers splayed over the other side. Pressing with her thumb, she turned Ben's head to the side, exposing the tempting expanse of her neck. She leaned forward and trailed her tongue along the pulse that beat heavily there.

Ben cradled Cori's head in her hands, her fingers tangling in her hair. She exerted enough pressure to tug Cori's head up sharply, but not enough to hurt. Sinking into the swirling depths of azure eyes hazy with passion, she somehow refrained from crushing her mouth against Cori's.

"How long do you intend to torture me?" Ben's mouth was inches from Cori's.

"Just long enough." Cori grinned before pressing her lips to Ben's.

The tentatively contained flame between them ignited with the first brush of their mouths. Ben sighed against Cori's lips as the thirst that had consumed her for weeks finally promised to be quenched. Wrapping her arms about Cori's neck, she pulled the taller woman against her, deepening the kiss. She tugged ineptly at the tuxedo shirt that was still between her own bare chest and Cori's skin.

Cori yanked the shirt open and shucked it off her shoulders. Ben's hands were back in her hair, pulling her mouth down. With Ben's tongue stroking inside her lips, it took all of Cori's waning concentration to fumble her own bra off. Dropping it behind her, she grasped Ben's hips and pulled their bodies flush, unsure which of them sighed as their skin met. Ben's thigh slid between hers, and the throbbing that had begun between her thighs became nearly intolerable.

Barely resisting the urge to thrust her hips against Ben's thigh, Cori propelled them toward the bed. Her plan to go slowly was virtually forgotten, but she managed to regain enough of her senses to grab Ben's hands just as they undid the fly on her pants.

"Let me." Ben's gently pleading tone was almost her undoing.

"Wait. If you touch me, I'll lose it."

"I know. I can feel how close you are. Let me."

Without waiting for a response, Ben pressed her hand flat against Cori's abdomen. She felt the muscles twitch. Her body surging with the power of Cori's reaction, she slipped her fingers lightly under the edge of Cori's waistband.

"Ben," Cori growled. When Ben's hand slid inside her panties, Cori's head dropped back. Her heart pounded and there was a rushing sound in her ears warning her that she was far too close to the edge. "Oh God, you're going to make me embarrass myself here."

"Shh, please," Ben hummed against her lips between kisses. "You're so amazing. Let me make you feel good." The last word came out on a half-moan as her fingers moved into warm wetness.

"Ah, baby—everything you do—makes me feel—ah—good." Cori struggled to form a coherent sentence. Her entire body spiraled inward, focused on Ben's fingers sliding against her.

Releasing her momentarily, Ben tugged Cori's pants and panties over her hips. She pushed them down around her ankles and urged her back to lie on the bed. Kneeling, she pulled off Cori's shoes and freed one leg, but she lost patience before she got to the other one.

She knew Cori was close, so when she lowered her mouth to the inside of her thighs she didn't linger before sliding upward. Pressing her tongue firmly against Cori's clitoris, she flattened her hand against Cori's stomach as her hips wrenched off the bed.

"Ben, I can't wait." Cori gasped out the warning through her teeth.

"I won't make you wait." Ben lifted her head only briefly as she slipped two fingers inside.

Matching the timing of her stroking tongue with the thrust of her fingers, she brought Cori quickly up, the pulsing muscles drawing her deeper. When each of Cori's moans became indistinguishable from the next and she panted with the effort of holding off her orgasm, Ben carried her over. She applied the slightest pressure against Cori's lower abdomen with one hand while curling the fingers inside. Cori's back bowed and she called out. Then she went limp, panting and whispering Ben's name.

As her breathing began to slow and her body gradually relaxed, Ben crawled up onto the bed next to Cori, still stroking her fingers lightly over her stomach, content simply to be touching her.

Cori rolled Ben onto her back and rose up over her. She reverently touched Ben's cheek. She had been fighting for control for so long that she had forgotten how amazingly sweet it could be to relinquish it. She stared in awe at the woman who had changed her life so completely and was suddenly compelled to tell her.

"Ben, I…" she began.

"Shh…"

Ben didn't need to hear it. She felt it in the protective way Cori's body curved over hers as she moved to cover her. She saw it in Cori's eyes, gazing at her—unshuttered. She didn't need Cori to put her feelings into words. When Cori relented and silently lowered her body onto Ben's, her gentle hands and insistently seeking lips conveyed her emotions.

❖

When Cori's fingertips trailed slowly over her buttocks, Ben moaned and rolled over. "You're going to kill me," she murmured groggily.

They had barely slept, instead spending most of the night learning every inch of each other's bodies. Ben was loath to waste a single moment of the time they were stealing together in an unconscious state, and she sensed that Cori felt the same. She didn't open her eyes for fear she would find herself alone and realize it had all been a dream.

When the aroma of coffee pervaded her senses, she couldn't hold out any longer. She pried open her eyes and blinked until she could focus. She was far too comfortable to move, lying stretched out on her stomach across the entire bed. Reluctantly she shifted onto her side. Cori sat perched on the edge of the bed.

"Good morning," she said smiling.

"Good morning." Ben sat up and reached for her hand. "I tend to be a bit of a bed hog," she confessed.

"I remembered." Cori was pleasantly surprised to realize that she had just spent a second full night with the same woman.

Ben's memory of their first night together rushed back as well. It was closely followed by that of Cori shutting herself in the bathroom and effectively shutting Ben out of her life. She wondered, now, if she would have to face that again. And she didn't know how she would survive it.

"Coffee?" Cori picked up two mugs from the nightstand and handed her one. "I would have made you breakfast but I don't know how you like your eggs."

Ben accepted the mug without a word.

"I'm not going anywhere," Cori said, reading the apprehension in her eyes.

"I—uh—"

"It's okay. I deserve your skepticism. Ben, you didn't want me to say this last night, but I love you."

"You don't have to—"

"But I do." Cori set aside their mugs and took Ben's hands in hers. "I'm sorry for the way I've treated you. I was trying so hard to be unselfish, for probably the first time in my life." She scoffed. "What you went through with your brother, I didn't want to be the one to put you through a moment's heartache."

"I wouldn't trade away the pain. It was something I was meant to go through. I was by his side when he needed me most, and that's what mattered." Ben pulled Cori closer, wrapping her arm around her, and waited while she settled against her side. "I love you. And I will be by your side for whatever you and I are meant to go through. If you'll let me."

"I will," Cori answered, her arm tightening around Ben's waist. She wasn't sure how she had gotten lucky enough to have a woman like Ben fall her for her, but God help her, she was going to hold on to her for as long as she could.

EPILOGUE

Cori opened the door to find Ben leaning against the doorjamb. She yanked her inside and kissed her thoroughly before even allowing her to put down her overnight bag. When they moved apart, they were both breathing heavily.

"Did you miss me?"

"Welcome back." They spoke at the same time.

"Darling, I was only gone for two days." Ben grabbed Cori's hand and pulled her toward the living room. Dropping her bag by the couch, she sat down and Cori settled beside her.

"How was your trip?" Cori asked.

"Uneventful. How was your meeting with Gretchen?"

"Very good. We're putting together a reception in a few weeks to award the scholarships for next fall."

"She's really enjoying being involved with the foundation, isn't she?"

"I think she likes it better than being my agent," Cori observed. "She's already talking about hiring an assistant to take care of the grunt work, you know, like managing my career, so she'll have more time for the foundation."

"Aw, you're not grunt work," Ben soothed. She pulled Cori's head to her shoulder and patted it patronizingly.

"I have a surprise for you." Cori beamed, unable to hold it in any longer.

Ben sighed. In the three months that they had been dating, she had been unable to convince Cori that it was not necessary to present her with a gift on a weekly basis. And as with everything she did, Cori certainly did not go halfway with her gifts. Ben absently fingered the diamond solitaire pendant at her neck, another of Cori's tokens.

Excitedly Cori reached into her pocket and pulled out a key, presenting it to Ben as if it was a precious bauble.

"A key? Sweetie, I've had a key to your apartment for weeks now." They'd had one made after Cori had gotten unexpectedly detained at a charity function. Ben had returned from out of town to find that Cori wasn't home yet and she had gone back to her apartment and crashed. Cori had insisted on the key, saying she wanted Ben to be there even if she was late.

"This is a key to the house upstate. I've been planning to spend more time up there, and now that things are settling down with the foundation, I want to move up there. Uh—I want us to move up there." She pushed her hand through her hair. "I'm messing this up. I'm asking you to move in with me—up there."

Ben smiled. This side of Cori that no one else saw never failed to charm her. In public Cori was smooth and polished and perfectly poised. Only Ben got to see the shy side.

"I would love to move up there with you."

Cori breathed an exaggerated sigh of relief. "I'm so glad you said yes."

"What did you do?" Ben's eyes narrowed suspiciously.

"I have another surprise." Cori stood and led Ben to the window. She pointed to the street.

"You didn't." Ben stared at the enormous SUV pulled up next to the curb. She remembered walking past it on the way in and wondering what idiot needed a vehicle that big in the city. *Turns out, I'm in love with the idiot.*

"Well, the Jag won't be practical if we're going to be spending most of our time upstate," Cori said.

"You traded the Jag for that blue monstrosity?"

"It's slate blue metallic, and it's not a monstrosity, it's a Hummer H2. *And* I didn't trade the Jag. I'm keeping my apartment in the city for when we need to be here, and it will stay garaged here."

Ben laughed.

"What's so funny?" Cori demanded.

"You are so adorable." Ben wrapped her arm around Cori's waist and hugged her.

"It has an air suspension package and off-road roof lamps," Cori mumbled defensively against Ben's neck, making her laugh harder.

About the Author

Born and raised in upstate New York, Erin Dutton now resides in Nashville, Tennessee. No longer a Yankee, and yet not a true Southerner, she remains somewhere between the two and is happy to claim both places as home. In her spare time she enjoys reading, golf, and riding her motorcycle.

Her story "Two Under Par" is included in the anthology *Erotic Interludes 5: Road Games*, and her second novel *Fully Involved* will be released by Bold Strokes Books in December 2007. For more information visit www.erindutton.com or e-mail erin@erindutton.com.

Books Available From Bold Strokes Books

Sequestered Hearts by Erin Dutton. A popular artist suddenly goes into seclusion, a reluctant reporter wants to know why, and a heart locked away yearns to be set free. (978-1-933110-78-3)

Erotic Interludes 5: Road Games, ed by. Radclyffe and Stacia Seaman. Adventure, "sport," and sex on the road—hot stories of travel adventures and games of seduction. (978-1-933110-77-6)

The Spanish Pearl by Catherine Friend. On a trip to Spain, Kate Vincent is accidentally transported back in time—an epic saga spiced with humor, lust, and danger. (978-1-933110-76-9)

Lady Knight by L-J Baker. Loyalty and honor clash with love and ambition in a medieval world of magic when female knight Riannon meets Lady Eleanor. (978-1-933110-75-2)

Dark Dreamer by Jennifer Fulton. Best-selling horror author Rowe Devlin falls under the spell of psychic Phoebe Temple. A Dark Vista romance. (978-1-933110-74-5)

Come and Get Me by Julie Cannon. Elliott Foster isn't used to pursuing women, but alluring attorney Lauren Collier makes her change her mind. (978-1-933110-73-8)

Blind Curves by Diane and Jacob Anderson-Minshall. Private eye Yoshi Yakamota comes to the aid of her ex-lover Velvet Erickson in the first Blind Eye mystery. (978-1-933110-72-1)

Dynasty of Rogues by Jane Fletcher. It's hate at first sight for Ranger Riki Sadiq and her new patrol corporal, Tanya Coppelli—except for their undeniable attraction. (978-1-933110-71-4)

Running With the Wind by Nell Stark. Sailing instructor Corrie Marsten has signed off on love until she meets Quinn Davies—one woman she can't ignore. (978-1-933110-70-7)

More Than Paradise by Jennifer Fulton. Two women battle danger, risk all, and find in each other an unexpected ally and an unforgettable love. (978-1-933110-69-1)

Flight Risk by Kim Baldwin. For Blayne Keller, being in the wrong place at the wrong time just might turn out to be the best thing that ever happened to her. (978-1-933110-68-4)

Rebel's Quest: Supreme Constellations Book Two by Gun Brooke. On a world torn by war, two women discover a love that defies all boundaries. (978-1-933110-67-7)

Punk and Zen by JD Glass. Angst, sex, love, rock. Trace, Candace, Francesca...Samantha. Losing control—and finding the truth within. BSB Victory Editions. (1-933110-66-X)

When Dreams Tremble by Radclyffe. Two women whose lives turned out far differently than they'd once imagined discover that sometimes the shape of the future can only be found in the past. (1-933110-64-3)

Stellium in Scorpio by Andrews & Austin. The passionate reuniting of two powerful women on the glitzy Las Vegas Strip, where everything is an illusion and love is a gamble. (1-933110-65-1)

The Devil Unleashed by Ali Vali. As the heat of violence rises, so does the passion. A Casey Clan crime saga. (1-933110-61-9)

Burning Dreams by Susan Smith. The chronicle of the challenges faced by a young drag king and an older woman who share a love "outside the bounds." (1-933110-62-7)

Fresh Tracks by Georgia Beers. Seven women, seven days. A lot can happen when old friends, lovers, and a new girl in town get together in the mountains. (1-933110-63-5)

The Empress and the Acolyte by Jane Fletcher. Jemeryl and Tevi fight to protect the very fabric of their world...time. Lyremouth Chronicles Book Three. (1-933110-60-0)

First Instinct by JLee Meyer. When high-stakes security fraud leads to murder, one woman flees for her life while another risks her heart to protect her. (1-933110-59-7)

Erotic Interludes 4: Extreme Passions, ed. by Radclyffe and Stacia Seaman. Thirty of today's hottest erotica writers set the pages aflame with love, lust, and steamy liaisons. (1-933110-58-9)

Unexpected Ties by Gina L. Dartt. With death before dessert, Kate Shannon and Nikki Harris are swept up in another tale of danger and romance. (1-933110-56-2)

Broken Wings by L-J Baker. When Rye Woods, a fairy, meets the beautiful dryad Flora Withe, her libido, as squashed and hidden as her wings, reawakens along with her heart. (1-933110-55-4)

Combust the Sun by Andrews & Austin. A Richfield and Rivers mystery set in L.A. Murder among the stars. (1-933110-52-X)

Sleep of Reason by Rose Beecham. Nothing is as it seems when Detective Jude Devine finds herself caught up in a small-town soap opera. And her rocky relationship with forensic pathologist Dr. Mercy Westmoreland just got a lot harder. (1-933110-53-8)

Grave Silence by Rose Beecham. Detective Jude Devine's investigation of a series of ritual murders is complicated by her torrid affair with the golden girl of Southwestern forensic pathology, Dr. Mercy Westmoreland. (1-933110-25-2)

Passion's Bright Fury by Radclyffe. When a trauma surgeon and a filmmaker become reluctant allies on the battleground between life and death, passion strikes without warning. (1-933110-54-6)

Tristaine Rises by Cate Culpepper. Brenna, Jesstin, and the Amazons of Tristaine face their greatest challenge for survival. (1-933110-50-3)

Of Drag Kings and the Wheel of Fate by Susan Smith. A blind date in a drag club leads to an unlikely romance. (1-933110-51-1)

Punk Like Me by JD Glass. Twenty-one-year-old Nina writes lyrics and plays guitar in the rock band Adam's Rib, and she doesn't always play by the rules. And oh yeah—she has a way with the girls. (1-933110-40-6)

Wild Abandon by Ronica Black. From their first tumultuous meeting, Dr. Chandler Brogan and Officer Sarah Monroe are drawn together by their common obsessions—sex, speed, and danger. (1-933110-35-X)

Chance by Grace Lennox. At twenty-six, Chance Delaney decides her life isn't working so she swaps it for a different one. What follows is the sexy, funny, touching story of two women who, in finding themselves, also find one another. (1-933110-31-7)

Turn Back Time by Radclyffe. Pearce Rifkin and Wynter Thompson have nothing in common but a shared passion for surgery. They clash at every opportunity, especially when matters of the heart are suddenly at stake. (1-933110-34-1)

Promising Hearts by Radclyffe. Dr. Vance Phelps lost everything in the War Between the States and arrives in New Hope, Montana, with no hope of happiness and no desire for anything except forgetting— until she meets Mae, a frontier madam. (1-933110-44-9)

Innocent Hearts by Radclyffe. In a wild and unforgiving land, two women learn about love, passion, and the wonders of the heart. (1-933110-21-X)

Justice Served by Radclyffe. Lieutenant Rebecca Frye and her lover, Dr. Catherine Rawlings, embark on a deadly game of hide-and-seek with an underworld kingpin who traffics in human souls. (1-933110-15-5)

Justice in the Shadows by Radclyffe. In a shadow world of secrets and lies, Detective Sergeant Rebecca Frye and her lover, Dr. Catherine Rawlings, join forces in the elusive search for justice. (1-933110-03-1)

A Matter of Trust by Radclyffe. JT Sloan is a cybersleuth who doesn't like attachments. Michael Lassiter is leaving her husband, and she needs Sloan's expertise to safeguard her company. It should just be business—but it turns into much more. (1-933110-33-3)

Fated Love by Radclyffe. Amidst the chaos and drama of a busy emergency room, two women must contend not only with the fragile nature of life, but also with the irresistible forces of fate. (1-933110-05-8)

Storms of Change by Radclyffe. In the continuing saga of the Provincetown Tales, duty and love are at odds as Reese and Tory face their greatest challenge. (1-933110-57-0)

Distant Shores, Silent Thunder by Radclyffe. Dr. Tory King—along with the women who love her—is forced to examine the boundaries of love, friendship, and the ties that transcend time. (1-933110-08-2)

Beyond the Breakwater by Radclyffe. One Provincetown summer, three women learn the true meaning of love, friendship, and family. (1-933110-06-6)

Safe Harbor by Radclyffe. A mysterious newcomer, a reclusive doctor, and a troubled gay teenager learn about love, friendship, and trust during one tumultuous summer in Provincetown. (1-933110-13-9)

shadowland by Radclyffe. In a world on the far edge of desire, two women are drawn together by power, passion, and dark pleasures. An erotic romance. (1-933110-11-2)

Love's Masquerade by Radclyffe. Plunged into the indistinguishable realms of fiction, fantasy, and hidden desires, Auden Frost is forced to question all she believes about the nature of love. (1-933110-14-7)

Honor Reclaimed by Radclyffe. In the aftermath of 9/11, Secret Service Agent Cameron Roberts and Blair Powell close ranks with a trusted few to find the would-be assassins who nearly claimed Blair's life. (1-933110-18-X)

Honor Guards by Radclyffe. In a wild flight for their lives, the president's daughter and those who are sworn to protect her wage a desperate struggle for survival. (1-933110-01-5)

Love & Honor by Radclyffe. The president's daughter and her lover are faced with difficult choices as they battle a tangled web of Washington intrigue for...love and honor. (1-933110-10-4)

Honor Bound by Radclyffe. Secret Service Agent Cameron Roberts and Blair Powell face political intrigue, a clandestine threat to Blair's safety, and the seemingly irreconcilable personal differences that force them ever farther apart. (1-933110-20-1)

Above All, Honor by Radclyffe. Secret Service Agent Cameron Roberts fights her desire for the one woman she can't have— Blair Powell, the daughter of the president of the United States. (1-933110-04-X)